# The Set Up

## R.J. Groves

# About the author

Australian author R.J. Groves has been passionate about writing since she could put pen to paper and can usually be found jotting plots and stories down on anything she can get her hands on. Describing herself as a mum, wife, author, and coffee lover, her other passions include music, cooking, books, adventures, and searching for plot bunnies in even the most mundane activities.

Facebook: facebook.com/rjgauthor
Instagram: instagram.com/r.j.groves_author
Twitter: twitter.com/rjg_author
Website: www.rjgrovesauthor.com

# Books by R. J. Groves

**The Bridal Shop series**
*Save the Date*
*Be My Valentine*
*Say You'll Be Mine*

**Jilted Brides series**
*Finding a Bride*
*Written in the Sand*

**Cities of the World series**
*In Paris*
*The Irish Maiden*

**Set Ups series**
*The Set Up*

**Mail Order Brides series**
*The Calm in the Storm*
*The Warmth in the Winter*
*The Song in the Silence*

**Standalones**
*Writing You*
*Two Babies Too Many*
*Second Chance*
*The Boyfriend Application*
*Sweeter Things*
*Home Bound*
*Stay With Me*
*Her First Noel*
*When Dreams Come True*
*To Fall For You*

For the single parent waiting for their happily ever
after.
Don't give up!

# The Set Up

R.J. Groves

# Chapter 1

'It's my day off.'

'I wouldn't be asking you if it wasn't.'

Brooke sighed, navigating her way through Bendigo's streets towards her mother's home. She was sure she sounded annoyed—she was. She only got two days off a week, and they were never in a row. Working in a jewellery store that was open every day made sure of that. And after she'd planned a full day of relaxing from anything work-related and spending time with her two adorable children, her dear mother Lily insisted she go in her place to help set up a birthday party. The last thing Brooke wanted to do was help someone she didn't know set up for a party.

'So, you're well enough to look after the kids, but

not to go to this party?' she said sarcastically, turning onto her mother's street.

'I have a migraine, darling. I'm not an invalid. Besides, I'm used to your children and Bill is home, so he can help. What I don't feel well enough to do is talk to a whole heap of people and pretend like I'm okay. But I promised Gladys I'd help set up. Your kids are quiet, at least.'

Brooke pulled into her mother's driveway and looked back at her kids. Maddie, her five-year-old daughter, was just about bursting out of her seat—she always enjoyed spending time with her grandparents. Ollie, her one-year-old son, was finally asleep. Unlike Maddie, Ollie had always been a clingy baby who still didn't sleep through the night. Last night was no exception. She'd spent the last hour driving around hoping he would have a sleep. She jumped out of the car just as her mother walked over to it.

'Tell her you're not feeling well, then,' Brooke said, hanging up the phone and opening Maddie's door to release her. 'I'm sure she'll manage.'

'Brooke, don't be selfish. I promised I would, and now I can't. So, I need you to go for me.' Her mother gave Maddie a cuddle and stood up straight again. 'She needs help.'

'I'll say,' Brooke scoffed, grabbing the kids backpacks from the car and dropping them on the ground near her mother. 'How old is her son?' She rounded the car to Ollie's door and carefully got him out. Despite trying to keep him asleep, he woke up and clung to her.

'Thirty-four.'

Brooke closed the door and walked back towards her mother and Maddie. 'And he can't throw his own damn party?'

'Don't swear in front of the children, Brooke,' Lily scolded.

'That's not swearing!' Maddie piped in. 'Mummy says—'

'Maddie,' Brooke warned, holding her finger up. The last thing she needed was for her children to tell her mother what other choice words she used.

Lily's eyes narrowed. 'Gladys is a good friend,' she said. 'And I've already told her you can go in my place.'

'Why would you say that?'

'Because I couldn't disappoint her completely.'

Brooke sighed, handing a reluctant Ollie over. 'Fine,' she groaned. 'I'll go this once. But don't go offering my services to any more of your friends. I like to enjoy my days off on occasion.'

She picked up the backpacks and followed her mum inside, Maddie running ahead to greet her pop, then returning to Brooke to get a kiss before she left. Brooke called out a greeting to her dad and waited for her mum to return with the invite. But when Lily came back into view, she was also carrying a dark blue floral dress with spaghetti straps and was short enough to be halfway up her thighs.

'What's this?'

Lily shoved the dress and the invite in her hands

and leaned Ollie close for a kiss. 'It's a dress,' she said flatly. 'You're not going in what you're wearing.'

Brooke's mouth dropped open and she glanced down at her comfortable jeans and tee she was wearing. 'What's wrong with this? I'm not going to help set up in a dress! Besides, this is Georgie's dress, not mine.' Georgie, Brooke's younger sister, spent half of her time travelling and half of her time saving at their parent's place.

'You two are the same size,' Lily said, waving her hand. 'You'll look fine.'

'I'm just setting up, right?' she said, nudging out the door before her mum signed her up for more.

'It would be rude not to stay,' Lily said, grabbing an envelope off the hall table, and adding it to the pile in Brooke's arms. 'For the birthday boy. You should go now, or you'll be late. Maddie! Come say goodbye to your mother.'

'Bye Mummy!' Maddie called out from inside the house.

'Be good!' she called back. Ollie started crying again and she pressed another kiss to his cheek. 'Mummy will be back soon.'

'Go, go!' Lily said, ushering her towards the car.

Brooke grumbled, climbing into her car, and starting it up. She looked down at the invite to find the address and grumbled again, shoving the dress and card to the passenger side. Of course, it was on the other side of town. She waved to her mum and the kids and reversed out of the driveway, heading in the right direction.

Surely a thirty-four-year-old man could manage to organise his own birthday party. It's not like it was one of the big ones that needed to be a surprise. Either way, she intended on only staying for as long as she had to. The second it seemed like she wasn't needed, she'd be out of there. She might even squeeze in a moment to herself before she picked up the kids. She scoffed. If only she were that lucky.

Being a parent was one thing. Being a single parent was another. And *that* was something she was still getting used to, even after a year and a half.

She double-checked the address when she turned onto the street, though she quickly realised she didn't need to. With blue and silver metallic-looking balloons tied to the mailbox, and people trekking back and forth between the delivery van and the house, it was pretty clear where the party was. It was only the biggest house in the street.

She pulled over as close as she could get to the house and gathered up the dress, rolling it into a ball and tucking it under her arm. Then, thinking better of it, she grabbed a canvas bag from the back of the car and put the dress in that. She got halfway to the house before she remembered the card. Swearing under her breath, she backtracked, grabbing the card off the passenger seat, and shoving it in the bag. Then she grabbed the invite for good measure and headed back towards the house, still annoyed at her mum for volunteering her to help.

Heading up the path towards the front door, she dodged a few caterers and fell into line behind them.

She scanned the inside of the house as she walked through, following the caterers to the kitchen. It wasn't a *huge* house, per se, though the front of the house gave that impression. Sure, the rooms were larger than usual, and it was furnished almost as though it was staged. There was barely any clutter. It reminded her mostly of a display home.

She could hear a woman giving orders from the kitchen and followed the sounds to find a middle-aged woman who was already dressed neatly enough for a party. She recognised Gladys—she'd met her once before at her parents' place when she dropped by one time. Gladys's eyes lit up when she saw Brooke and rushed over to plant a kiss on her cheek—an action Brooke never really understood, but she politely accepted it.

'Brooke, darling, you made it!' Gladys said. 'Lily rung to tell me you were on your way, I was hoping you'd find the place all right.'

'Hard to miss it,' she said, trying to make sure the annoyance wasn't obvious in her tone. 'You have a beautiful home, Mrs Rieder.'

Gladys waved her hand dismissively. 'Thank you,' she said. 'And please, it's Gladys. You're not a child.'

Brooke nodded. Truth is, she always called people by their title, especially if they were older than her. She'd been taught to do it as a child to show respect and, well, she guessed she never really grew out of it. She could understand how it might seem weird now, though. It was one of the things she still had to work on.

She nodded. 'All right, Gladys,' she said. 'Mum said you need help. With setting up, I mean. For the party.'

She cringed at the way she spoke. Perhaps it was the lack of clutter around the house that made her uncomfortable. It was very unlike her cluttered home. Then again, most of her clutter belonged to her kids. And children—especially young ones—come with a lot of it. It's practically unavoidable.

'Yes, please. This way!' Gladys led the way out the back door.

The door led onto a deck with a beautiful view of the town. On the deck were a few outdoor couches and a table that had been pushed up against the wall and covered with champagne glasses and a few empty metal tubs—the drinks table, she suspected. Gladys led the way off the deck into the backyard that was like walking through the Australian version of an English garden. There was an open grassy area with plastic chairs stacked in a pile at the edge. There were paved paths leading away from the open area that were lined with raised garden beds—bushes and hedges tall enough to provide some privacy in a garden walk. Being late springtime, the whole garden was filled with flowers of all colours and it looked truly beautiful. Gladys's voice snapped her out of her thoughts.

'I need these chairs spread around this grassy area,' Gladys said.

She continued to give instructions of how she wanted the chairs to be set up—around the open area in groups to encourage conversation, but close enough to the edges to still allow for mingling in the middle. A few fold-up tables were to be put near the edge of the deck for food. When Gladys reached what she hoped was the last of the instructions, a curly brown-haired girl about the same size as Maddie bounced out from the garden and gave Gladys a hug. She looked up at Brooke with her big brown eyes and smiled a toothy grin. She threw her little hand out in front of her towards Brooke.

'I'm Gracie,' she said. 'Who are you?'

Brooke crouched down until she came to Gracie's level and took the girl's hand in hers. 'I'm Brooke,' she said, glancing up at Gladys. 'Is this your nan?'

Gracie nodded animatedly, the curls piled on top of her head in a ponytail bobbing. 'Do you have kids?'

'I do,' Brooke said.

'Are they here?'

Brooke shook her head. 'They're with their nan and pop today.'

'Gracie, this is a grown-up party,' Gladys said. 'There won't be any other kids coming.'

Gracie made an exasperated groan and dropped her head. Then, as though she got over the disappointment quicker than it came, she glanced up at Brooke again, her eyes dancing. 'It's my dad's birthday party, you know,' she said, matter-of-factly.

Brooke raised an eyebrow. 'Oh, really?' she said. 'I bet you've been excited for it, then.'

She nodded, smiling. Gladys cleared her throat.

'Well, Gracie, why don't you help Brooke set up the chairs down here while I sort out the caterers?' Gladys said.

'Okay, Nanna!' Gracie bounced over to Brooke and took hold of her hand.

Without a second glance, Gladys started powering towards the house to instruct the caterers some more. Brooke released a deep breath she didn't realise she'd been holding onto and felt a tug on her hand. She looked down at the big brown eyes staring up at her.

'We should do what Nanna says,' Gracie said. 'Do you know what to do?'

Brooke raised an eyebrow. 'Do *you*?'

Gracie squinted. 'I'm only five. What do you think?'

Brooke nodded slowly. This kid was clever. She pointed to the piles of chairs. 'We need to move those chairs over there.'

She pointed to certain spots on the open area as she spoke, wondering how on earth a small five-year-old was going to be much help. She knew Maddie couldn't lift a chair—she only dragged. And she suspected Gladys wouldn't be very happy with her lawn being torn up. She lifted a chair off the pile and placed it near Gracie, lifting another off for herself. As she suspected might have happened, Gracie emphatically tried to lift the chair, grunting, and making all kinds of childish noises.

'Need a hand?' Brooke said, holding her chair with one hand on the back of it.

Gracie nodded, so she held onto one side of the chair while Gracie held the other. It was more awkward than anything, but Brooke knew how kids like to help. She knew it all too well.

'How old are your kids?' Gracie said.

'Maddie is five, and Ollie, my boy, has just turned one.'

Gracie's eyes lit up at the mention of Maddie. 'I'm five!'

'Really?' she said, trying to feign interest. 'I thought you were about the same height as Maddie.'

'You should have brought her,' Gracie said. 'So I have someone to play with. I don't like grown-up parties.'

Brooke's brow furrowed. 'Do you go to many grown-up parties?'

Gracie shook her head, the curls bobbing. 'No, but they don't sound like much fun.'

Brooke smiled, laughing a little as they put the chairs down next to each other. 'Well, if I knew you were going to be here, I might have brought Maddie with me. Maybe another time.'

She didn't intend on there being another time at one of these things, but if Gladys was Gracie's Nanna, then there was the possibility she was looking after her at the same time as Maddie being with Brooke's mum. The possibility of a playdate didn't sound so foreign. As long as she wasn't expected to be there on one of her days off.

They'd only just finished setting up when people started arriving, and Brooke took it as her cue to leave. Still dressed in her jeans and tee, she did not fit in with the dress code of the new arrivals. She hunted down Gladys and waited until she'd finished greeting one of the party-goers—a pretty brunette dressed a bit too fancy for a house party. Then again, this was a rather different house party, it seemed, with catering instead of pizza, set seating areas, and champagne. Oh, and no kids except for the one that belongs to the birthday boy. Who, by the way, was still yet to make an appearance.

Gladys finished talking to the brunette and turned towards her, looking her up and down with a scowl. Brooke smiled, which she was afraid looked more like a grimace. 'Why haven't you changed yet?'

Brooke's eyebrow shot up. What was wrong with how she looked? 'I should go, Gladys,' she said. 'Unless there's something else you need me to do?'

Gladys grabbed hold of her arm, looking around, and scuttled her towards a closed door. 'Nonsense,' Gladys said. 'You have to stay. Lily said you would stay.' *Damn Lily.* 'I moved your bag into the spare room—I hope you don't mind. You can get changed in there.' She swung the door open and pushed her into the room. 'Get dressed and come enjoy the party.' Gladys left, closing the door behind her.

Brooke sighed. It seemed it was going to be harder than she thought to escape. But she supposed it wasn't so bad. Sure, she didn't particularly *want* to be there. And she was annoyed at her mother for volunteering her to help set up and saying she'd stay for the party, too. But she supposed she could *try* to enjoy it. After all, it wasn't often when she was kid-free on her day off.

***

'Mum! I've got the ice!'

Lewis eased his way into his mother's house. It was beginning to fill with people who he did not recognise very quickly. He pushed his way past a caterer to get to the kitchen where his mother was bound to be barking orders at some poor soul. He found her busying herself with telling a caterer to keep making the rounds until all the food was off her tray instead of coming back to the kitchen.

'Mum,' he said, drawing out the syllables. Gladys looked at him, scowling. He held up the bags of ice he'd been sent out to get.

'Where have you been?' she said, dropping her hands onto her hips. 'I sent you to get ice over an hour ago.'

He raised an eyebrow. 'Well, seems you picked a *terrible* day to want ice because I had to go to almost every service station in Bendigo to get some. Where do you want it?'

She waved towards the back door. 'The ice buckets on the drinks table. The poor souls that are already here have had to make do with warm champagne. Then go get dressed—you *are* the birthday boy, after all.'

'I'm sure they'll manage,' he said, heading through the door.

There were more people out the back mingling. Some sitting awkwardly next to each other but not conversing. He frowned. He knew none of them and he was starting to notice a pretty noticeable fact about the party guests—aside from him, his two best friends, and a few caterers, they were all women. He dumped the bags of ice on the floor near the drinks table and opened a bag, filling one of the ice buckets. Then, he opened another and casually tipped it into the other bucket. He put the other bag of ice in the esky underneath the table.

'So, a birthday party, huh?'

'Where's the beer and sports?'

Lewis smiled at his friends as they came up onto the deck. Drew and Miles had been Lewis's friends for years. They all worked as building contractors and, more often than not, worked on the same houses together. They'd always been good for a lark, but scenes like this were usually out of their comfort zones. Saying that, scenes like this were out of *his* comfort zone. At least they'd listened to the one instruction he'd given them about dressing neatly.

'Not that we're complaining,' Drew said, running a hand through his short brown hair. 'With all the women here and the obvious shortage of guys.'

'But do you actually *know* all these women?' Miles said, shaking his head. His blond hair that usually fell over his face like a mop was combed to the side. He might not have recognised his friends if they hadn't been the only other guys here. And if he hadn't known them for so long.

'I can honestly say I have *no* idea who any of these women are,' Lewis said, squinting as he scanned the growing crowd. The women all seemed to be around the same age. He was definitely seeing a pattern here.

'Isn't it your party, dude?' Miles said.

Lewis shook his head slowly. 'I'll ask Mum what's going on. But for now, I have to get changed— Mother's orders,' he mumbled, heading back inside. Though he felt like he already knew the answer.

He shook his head when he went into the spare bedroom that Gracie sometimes stayed in and saw his clothes laid out on the bed. *Of course,* his mother wanted a say in what he wore, too. He shrugged the clothes on and sprayed some cologne, shoving his worn clothes into his bag and dropping it on the ground near the bed. Hoping his mother would be happy enough with his presentation, he left the room and started searching for Gladys.

After scanning the rooms as he walked through them towards the backyard, he finally caught sight of her near the drinks table, pouring some champagne for one of the guests. As he reached the door, he glanced back to the dining table that had clearly been the designated presents table. God, it was like being a kid again. But he didn't care much for the presents, since they mostly came from people he didn't know. What caught his eye was the slender blonde he saw slipping an envelope onto the pile.

A few inches shorter than him, her hair held high in a ponytail, draping down to just below the middle of her shoulders in thick wavy ringlets. She wore a dark blue dress that hugged her body in all the right places. And on her feet, she wore … runners? He felt his eyebrow flick up in amusement. Either she detested wearing heels *that* much, or she wasn't prepared. Either way, she looked a whole lot more appealing than any other of the strangers at the party.

But she would have to wait.

Seeing a break in conversation between Gladys and the lady she'd poured some champagne for, he took the opportunity before there were any more people to distract her.

'Mother, a word,' he said, grabbing hold of her arm, and pulling her away from the lady.

'Lewis, whate—'

He turned to face her. 'What's going on, *Mother*?'

Gladys lifted her chin, her lips tight, but something flashed in her eyes that he couldn't quite place. She was up to something. 'I don't know what you're talking about.'

He groaned. 'The party, Mum,' he said. 'And the fact it's filled with a whole lot of people—women—who I don't know. Does that ring a bell?'

Her lips curved to the side. 'Honey, it's been five years.'

*Oh, no.* Not this again. He pinched the bridge of his nose, catching a glimpse of the runners woman sneaking out the back door and down the balcony steps. 'We've been through this.'

Gladys held onto his arm, concern on her face.

'Lewis, honey, I just want to see you happy.'

'I *am* happy, Mother.'

'Gracie needs a mother.'

'No,' he said flatly. 'Gracie needs me, and she needs her Nanna.'

'Well, I'm not going to be around forever, you know.'

His brow furrowed. 'Are you … sick?'

'No, I am not,' Gladys said. 'But my point is the same. She needs a mother.'

'She needs her Nanna to stop meddling with her father's love life.'

'Well, it's too late now,' Gladys said. 'Everyone's already here. And they're all here for *you*, dear boy.' She gave him a pat on his arm. 'So, make the most of it. There's no harm in looking at your options.' She grabbed hold of a tall brunette passing by. 'Have you met Annalise, yet? Annalise, this is my son, Lewis.'

'The birthday boy,' the woman said, extending her hand, and batting her eyelids. 'A pleasure.'

He nodded, shaking her hand lazily and grabbing a drink from the table. He finished the glass in one gulp and filled it up again, shooting a look towards his friends. He could see the party wasn't what they'd expected it to be, but they, at least, seemed to be enjoying being surrounded by pretty women.

'What do you do, Annalise?' he said, taking a sip of his second glass.

'I'm a model,' she said, almost robotically.

He took another big sip, watching as his mother talked to another woman—with dyed blonde hair and a skimpy dress—and pointed up towards him. 'Are you enjoying the party?'

She nodded, smiling, though her expression didn't change much. 'I like parties like this. I much prefer them … without … kids, though.'

He frowned, following her gaze to see Gracie running around in the garden. She looked cute in her puffy dress and stockings. Gladys wouldn't be happy she'd ditched her shoes and was getting her stockings dirty, but the thought made him smile.

'That would be *my* child,' he said, looking back at Annalise.

Her eyes widened, and she dropped her gaze. 'Sorry … I—'

'Excuse me. Lewis, do you mind if I steal you for a chat?'

The blonde talking to Gladys had made her way next to them and had hold of Lewis's arm. He felt his jaw set. He could tell what his mother was up to and he didn't like it. Nor did he approve of it. He was quite capable of finding a woman himself *if* he was looking for one. Which he wasn't. But good luck trying to convince Gladys. Head low, Annalise left him with the blonde.

'I'm Jennifer,' she said, holding her hand out to him.

He took it and she swept in to kiss him on the cheek, her hair whacking him in the face as she did. He was never used to the custom of cheek-kissing upon meeting, but his mother seemed to be all for it. But getting closer to the blonde *did* give him the chance to notice something he otherwise might not have—she looked young.

'How old are you, Jennifer?' he asked.

'I just turned twenty.'

*Twenty*? Holy smokes. He was almost old enough to be her father! If he had managed to get some poor girl pregnant as a teenager, that is. He downed the rest of his glass and got another. He could see he was in for a long night. He grabbed a bottle of champagne and started walking off the deck to the gardens, Jennifer babbling his ears off about … something. He wasn't sure what. He was still stuck on the fact she was still basically a kid.

# Chapter 2

It's like a bloody cocktail party on *The Bachelor*. Women were beelining towards him left, right, and centre, while Brooke tried her best to blend in with the furniture. It was obvious the guy—Lewis, so she'd heard—knew none of the women at the party. And it didn't take her long to work out Gladys had an ulterior motive for the party. And it wasn't long after that she realised her own mother might have had an ulterior motive. *Go in my place*? She was calling bull on that one. Lily never intended on going to this party—she'd always planned on Brooke taking her place.

She took a sip of her drink and sunk further into the couch that had, at some point, been moved down off the deck to the edge of the grassy area. She suspected it must have been while she was getting changed. She crossed her legs as politely as one could when they were practically laying on the couch and stared at her shoes. Runners. The same shoes she was wearing with her jeans and tee, except they suited those clothes better than Georgie's sundress.

And on *that* topic, she was *not* the same size as Georgie. Georgie hadn't popped out any kids yet— she was yet to fill out in the hip region as Brooke had. They might *wear* similarly sized clothing, but dresses that draped on Georgie hugged Brooke a little too close for her comfort. Which is probably one of the many reasons why she rarely wore dresses. The biggest reason was that dresses— especially short ones—are entirely impractical with small kids. Another reason was that you have to sit a whole lot more ladylike than what becomes the usual mum sitting arrangement.

Brooke chuckled to herself. She could feel the champagne going to her head—another thing that was very different since becoming a mum. She could *not* hold her liquor as well as she used to. She felt her eyes drift towards Lewis as another woman vied for his attention. He'd had more drinks than her— she did have to drive home, after all—but he seemed to be more uncomfortable than anything with the whole situation. Probably a lot like she was. God, she would be giving her mum an earful for tricking her into coming to this damn thing.

She finished off her glass and handed it to a caterer walking past with a tray full of dirty glasses and sunk back into the couch, closing her eyes. The sun had a bite to it today, but the couch was somewhat in the shade, so she was able to enjoy a nice breeze. And even though she was alone, she found her mind drifting to her kids. God, if she wasn't with them, she was thinking about them. She supposed it came with being a mother. She felt a tug on her arm and opened her eyes to be met with the big brown eyes that had disappeared for a few hours.

'Can I sit with you?' Gracie said.

Brooke nodded and sat up straighter to allow enough room for Gracie to share the couch. 'Are you enjoying the party?'

Gracie bit into her lip and shook her head. 'All the ladies are really pretty but no one wants to talk to me.'

Brooke frowned, her heart aching for the girl. She was starting to wish more and more that she actually knew more about the party before coming. She could have brought Maddie with her. At least Gracie would have had someone to play with, then. Even if Brooke still didn't want to be there.

'I saw you running around in the garden,' she said. 'Was that fun?'

Gracie dropped her gaze. 'I was trying to get some ladies to play with me, but they didn't want to.'

Gracie shifted in the seat, so her shoulder brushed against Brooke's. Brooke nudged her gently. 'Oh, I bet that's because they knew they couldn't keep up with you in their high heels.'

She thought she saw a little smile tug at her lips

before Gracie glanced up at her. 'But *you* could!' she said excitedly, pointing to her shoes. 'You're not wearing high heels!'

Brooke smiled, pointing to Gracie's stained stockings. 'And you're not wearing any.'

'Will you play with me, Brooke? Oh, please?' Gracie pouted, her eyes rounding into the best impersonation of puppy-dog eyes she'd ever seen.

She sighed. She hadn't *wanted* to do anything, really. But heck, the idea of playing a little game in the garden with Gracie sounded like the most fun she was going to have at this party. And if she couldn't bring Maddie, the least she could do was make sure Gracie got to enjoy her dad's birthday party at least a little.

'Sure, honey,' she said, standing when Gracie leapt to her feet and pulled on her arm. She was glad she was wearing runners, after all. If she'd been wearing heels, she'd be worried she might not have kept her balance. 'Lead the way.'

Still holding Brooke's hand, Gracie weaved them through the crowd towards the garden until they came to a flattened stump that had a little tea-set arranged on it. She smiled at the thought of how much fun Maddie would have here and wondered at the possibility of a playdate after all. She was sure Lily and Gladys could work something out. She'd have to talk to her meddling mother when she picked up the children.

Gracie pretended to pour a cup of tea for Brooke and handed the little cup and saucer to her. It was actually like taking a breath of fresh air, being away from the party a little. It was refreshing.

'What's Maddie like?' Gracie said, sipping her own pretend cup of tea.

'Well,' Brooke said, tilting her head to the side. 'She has blonde hair—curls, a bit like yours.'

'Is her hair the same colour as yours?'

'Similar,' she said, thoughtfully. 'But hers is lighter. Mine is more of a darker blonde. Have you ever seen hay?' Gracie nodded. 'Her hair looks a little like the colour of hay. Mine is closer to …' She drifted off, trying to think of something to compare it to. Honestly, she hadn't paid much attention to her hair colour in that much detail.

'Yours looks like honey,' Gracie offered.

Brooke smiled. 'Honey,' she repeated. 'We'll go with that.'

'Tell me more.' Gracie grabbed a plastic muffin from the plate in the middle of the stump and handed one to Brooke. She pretended to eat it to amuse her.

'Well,' she continued. 'She's about your height. She likes wearing pretty dresses and running around outside.'

'Would she like me, do you think?' Gracie batted her eyelids like she'd seen many of the women at the party do to Lewis.

'I'm sure she would love you, Gracie,' she said.

Gracie smiled and jumped to her feet. 'Does she like flowers?' she said, spinning around in lazy circles near the bright flowers in the garden.

'She loves flowers.'

Gracie smiled and leapt with excitement, but the excitement quickly turned into a scream as her face reddened and she started hopping on one foot, clutching her other. Brooke jumped to her feet, her eyes dropping to where Gracie's foot had landed, just in time to see a bee dizzily flying away. *Shoot.* She swore under her breath as she rushed over to Gracie and the small girl grabbed onto her arm.

'Can you walk, honey? Are you allergic?'

'What ... does ... that ... m–mean?' Gracie said between sobs.

*Shoot.* She could see she wasn't going to get a clear answer from Gracie. She bent down closer to her level. 'I'm going to pick you up, okay? We need to get you inside to look at the owwie.'

Gracie nodded, flinging her arms around Brooke's neck. She lifted her up and started rushing her towards the house, praying to God the kid wasn't allergic. *That* would really put a downer on the party. And already she felt guilty for even being near the girl when she got hurt.

***

Lewis scanned his surroundings when he heard the scream, his heart thumping hard in his chest. *Gracie.* He put his glass and the champagne bottle on a vacant chair and craned his neck to get a better view, ignoring the woman who was trying to tell him about ... whatever it was she was trying to say. He'd pretty much lost interest in the whole scenario and had drifted to nodding and making the occasional noises to seem like he was interested. He could still hear Gracie's sobbing but couldn't see her.

'Are you even listening?' the woman said, annoyed.

'Sorry,' he mumbled. 'It's just I—my kid is crying, and I can't—'

'Wait, you have a *kid*?'

He scowled at the disgusted look on the woman's face. It seemed to be the flavour of the day. 'Yes, I am a father. Is that a problem?'

He swore under his breath, pushing past her to follow the sound. Fancy the majority of the women his mother invited to the party being turned off by the fact he was a father. In fact, he'd be willing to bet *none* of these women even had kids—let alone had any experience with kids. Through a gap in the crowd, he could see Gracie's head bobbing as she was being rushed towards the house—*carried* towards the house. She was crying, and he felt a wave of terror wash over him as he chased the blonde-haired woman carrying his child. God, if she had any ulterior motives with his kid, he would—

'What the *hell* is going on here?' he said, grabbing hold of the woman's shoulder.

Gracie let out another cry and the woman turned towards him, almost throwing him off balance with the intensity in her eyes. They were rounded, wide, and the colour was almost amber—somewhere between the colour of red-box honey and whisky.

The way the sun shone on her hair made it look more golden than blonde. Then, he realised her expression was more worried than anything.

'You're her father, right?' she said, hurriedly. He nodded, finding himself at a loss for words. 'Good,' she continued, passing Gracie into his arms. 'We have to get her up to the house, quickly.'

He was about to ask why, but Gracie started crying some more and the blonde had already started pulling them towards the house. He didn't need to be told twice. He took the steps up to the balcony two at a time and pushed through the back door into the kitchen.

'On the bench,' the woman said, clearing a spot on the bench. 'Take her stockings off,' she said, starting to open and close cupboard doors. 'Is she allergic to bees?'

He sat Gracie on the bench and started rolling her stockings down, starting with the foot Gracie was holding on to, and was met with a red welt on her foot. 'I'm not—I don't—what the *hell* is going on?'

'She's been stung by a bee!' she said, exasperated, spinning to face him. 'Is she allergic or not?'

He shook his head. 'I wouldn't know. She's never been stung before.'

Her eyes widened. 'She's five and she's never been stung before?' He shook his head. She returned to banging the cupboard doors. 'Maddie got her first sting when she was two. Ollie's been walking for a month and he's already been stung.' She closed the last cupboard door. 'God, does your mother keep an antiseptic cream anywhere logical?'

He shook his head again. 'I wouldn't know. We could ask—'

'No time,' she said, rubbing her forehead. 'Vinegar? Surely, she'd have vinegar.' She turned to the pantry and retrieved a bottle of apple cider vinegar and a jar of honey. She came around to stand in front of Gracie, grabbing the tissue box as she passed it, and lifted her foot to get a better look. 'This might hurt, darling,' she said softly.

She ran her fingernail over the welt, Gracie crying again, then wiped her fingernail on a tissue. Lewis could see the stinger on the tissue as she continued working. She folded another tissue and tipped some vinegar on it, pressing the wet tissue to the sting on Gracie's foot. She looked up at him, the amber of her eyes looking warmer than it had moments ago.

'The vinegar acts as an antiseptic,' she explained. 'And it seems to neutralise bee venom. The honey helps with the itching and helps it heal quickly.'

'How do you know that?' he said.

She removed the vinegar-soaked tissue and smoothed some honey over the sting. 'I told you, Maddie and Ollie—'

'*Who* are they?'

'They're my kids,' she said, frowning at him before focussing back on Gracie. 'Maddie's five, Ollie's one.'

She was a mother? Well, that explained why he'd seen Gracie hanging around her. She was probably the only woman here who understood the poor child. Then, on the other hand, if she was a mother of children so young, what was she doing here?

'Wh—what are you doing here?' he said. 'At the party, I mean.'

She laughed softly, a sound that seemed to vibrate through his whole body. 'I was wondering the same thing,' she mumbled. 'My meddling mother, I suppose. She volunteered my services to help set up. I didn't realise I was expected to stay. Hence the runners.'

He smiled down at her shoes. 'I did wonder about them,' he said. She glanced up at him, her expression unreadable. Surprise, perhaps? He thought he could see her cheeks darken as she dropped her gaze to focus on Gracie's foot. Gracie had stopped crying and was looking worriedly at her foot as well. 'It seems they came in handy, though. Having to carry Gracie halfway to the house and all.'

She smiled again. 'I suppose it's just as well I stayed, then, too,' she added. 'I'm pretty sure none of those other women would know how to deal with a bee sting on a child's foot.' She looked up at him. 'No offence.'

He raised an eyebrow. 'None taken,' he said, leaning against the bench. 'Honestly, I was kind of suspecting that myself.'

Her smile widened, but her lips were pressed together as though trying not to laugh. She stood up straight, putting her hands on her hips, and sighing. A few beads of perspiration lined her forehead and some of her hair had come out of her ponytail. A few freckles spattered her nose, but it only made her look even more beautiful. She brushed the hairs out of her face, but he couldn't help but notice the urge to do it himself.

Who was this woman?

He focussed back on Gracie, hoping the woman didn't notice he'd been staring at her for longer than he should have, and nudged her shoulder. 'How are you feeling, noodle?'

Gracie's cheeks darkened, and her eyes went wide. 'Da-ad,' she said, drawing his name out. 'Not in front of Brooke.'

His mouth dropped open. 'Since when have you ever been embarrassed?' It was easy enough to assume the beautiful blonde standing next to him was Brooke. *Brooke*. It was a nice name. He felt his heart skip a beat, an irrational response to a name.

'Since I *like* her,' Gracie said. 'She's way better than any of the other ladies here. I don't like anyone else. I like *her*.'

He glanced up at Brooke, catching her eyes with his. Her eyes were wide, and her face had paled. What was she playing at? He'd come to realise every woman at this party seemed to know his mother had intended it to be a matchmaking event. Surely, Brooke wasn't the only one at the party who didn't know. She had to be pretending. And she'd taken a different approach to the rest of the women at the party. She went through his kid. And now, his kid was going to be disappointed thanks to this cunning wench.

'I … umm … I should…' she stammered, pursing her lips as though trying to think of what to say.

Admittedly, it looked cute. But he wasn't going to be fooled by her tactics. He'd told his mother he wasn't looking for someone, and he'd tell anyone else the same thing. Including her. Even if she had made a lasting impression on him. Even if he wouldn't be able to stop thinking about her. He crossed his arms over his chest.

'What on earth is going on here?' Gladys said, coming into the kitchen. 'Is Gracie all right?'

'Bee sting, Mother,' he said, holding Brooke's gaze for a moment longer before she looked away. She stared at the ground, sucking her lips in, pressing them together in a thin line. He turned his gaze to his mother. 'She's okay, though. Doesn't look like she's allergic, but we should keep an eye on her. Brooke seemed to know what she was doing.'

Brooke glared up at him before focussing on Gladys, a forced smile on her face. 'She'll need some more honey on it in a little while,' she said. 'And you might like to bandage it, so it doesn't rub off on all your nice things.'

Gladys gathered Gracie up in her arms and held her close. 'Thank you, Brooke.'

Brooke nodded, dropping her gaze again. 'I should … umm … I have to go. Sorry, Gladys. It's a lovely party, but I … I'm not feeling well.'

She rubbed her forehead, and she squinted as if trying to emphasise her point. It was lies. All lies. He knew she felt fine. Except she probably realised he knew what she was up to. His mother didn't notice how fake it was.

Gladys nodded, her brow furrowing in concern. 'Of course, darling. Tell Lily I'll call in on her tomorrow.'

Brooke nodded. 'I will, thank you.' She started backing towards the front door.

Gladys whacked Lewis on the arm to get his attention. 'See her out, won't you?' she said. 'I'll go find a bandage for Gracie.'

Brooke's eyes widened again. 'Oh, no,' she said. 'I can see myself out. I'll just get my things and be on my way.' She nudged open the door to the spare room and plucked out a canvas bag from just inside the door and held it up. 'Thanks, Gladys.'

She turned and started walking quickly towards the front door. Lewis felt another whack against his arm.

***

Brooke felt like she couldn't get out of there quickly enough. She stepped through the front door, pausing only to take a quick breath before she started walking again. What the hell happened in there? She'd thought she'd seen something in his eyes. Relief, maybe. Probably because he realised there was actually someone who was in a similar situation at the party, as opposed to all those young, model-like women who were all pretty and probably had no idea how to deal with kids.

It had stirred something inside her. Something she hadn't felt before. The kind of something that made her blush uncontrollably, her hairs stand on end, and made her feel nervous. She didn't *feel* nervous. She never did. She was straight to the point, worked well under pressure, and didn't put up with any nonsense. Nervous wasn't her. And one look from the guy had her knees week and her head light.

Then the look had changed.

And it made her uncomfortable. As though he was analysing her, comparing her, even. Looking at her the same way as he looked at all those other women. She reached the street and turned in the direction of her car. She heard the front door swing open and close and started walking faster. Her car seemed much further away than she remembered it being and she whispered to herself.

'Please, don't let it be him,' she whispered, squeezing her eyes shut for a brief second. 'Please, please, *please* don't—'

'Hold up, Brooke.'

*Damn it.* Reluctantly, she stopped, opening her eyes to see she'd almost reached her car. She heard his footsteps slowing down, but they were still heavy. Purposeful.

'We need to talk.'

She turned to face him, startling at his closeness. God, had he thrown her senses off so much she hadn't even realised how *close* he was standing behind her? His eyes were narrowed, his brow furrowed.

She shook her head. 'N—no, we don't.'

She lifted the handles of the canvas bag onto her shoulder instead of hooked on her arm. Then, she felt like it was probably more awkward than having it on her arm. But she wasn't about to give him the satisfaction of knowing he made her nervous and self-conscious.

'Oh, yes, we do.' He indicated towards the car next to them. 'Is this your car?'

She studied his face for a moment, then shook her head, sighing. She couldn't believe she was about to do this, but she absently waved her hand towards the next car down the street that *was* her car. She hoped she wouldn't regret it. She knew how guys were with their cars. She knew he'd probably recognise her car anywhere, now. Brett had been able to. And at first, she'd thought it was an endearing feature. Then, she grew to regret it.

He held onto her arm—gentle, but firm at the same time—and led her towards her car. 'Get in.'

Her mouth dropped open and she shook his hand off her arm. '*Excuse me?*'

He sighed, rubbing his forehead. 'I want to talk *without* being interrupted for the first time at this ... thing. And unless we're in your car, that's not going to happen.'

She considered him again, wondering what kind of game he was playing. She still wasn't sure about the whole having a stranger in the same car as her. And she certainly didn't like being ordered around.

But he wasn't *entirely* a stranger. He was her mother's best friend's son. He should be okay, right? She unlocked the car and moved around to the driver side, shooting up a silent prayer she wouldn't regret this. He got in the passenger side and she quickly realised how the air seemed to be sucked out of the car once he was in. She fiddled with the keys in her hands and looked at him.

'What is it?' she prompted.

'I want to know what you're getting at.'

The words were cold, matter-of-fact. Bored? She was taken aback. 'What *I'm* getting at?' she said, her pitch a little higher than normal. 'How about what *you're* getting at!'

'What's *that* supposed to mean?' He glared at her, annoyance clear on his face.

She waved towards the house. 'That whole scene. Who gets his mother to throw a party for them to serve as a ... a ... *Bachelor.*'

His eyebrow's lifted. '*What*?'

'You know, *The Bachelor*,' she explained. 'Heaps of girls, one guy. Everyone vying for his attention and dying to be noticed.'

He shook his head. 'I didn't *ask* for that. My mother took it into her own hands to try to find me a wife. I was happy with how things already are.' He shifted in his seat to face her better. 'Might I remind you *you're* the one that *came* to the party.'

She scoffed. 'Against my will.' His brow furrowed, and she continued. '*My* mother told me she'd promised Gladys she'd help set up for the party, then feigned being sick and said I had to go in her place because she didn't want to disappoint *your* mother. I didn't plan on staying, but your mother insisted.'

His eyebrow raised in amusement. 'So, you were tricked into coming to the party?'

'Unfortunately,' she mumbled, staring down at the keys in her hands. Her knuckles were white, and she took a shaky breath. 'But it didn't take me long to realise there was a particular theme to the party.'

'But you still stayed,' he pointed out.

She shrugged. 'Selfish reasons, I guess,' she said. His eyes widened. '*Not* that,' she added. 'I don't get much … me … time. I figured even if I wasn't particularly enjoying the party it was still a break from the usual. Then, I saw how sad Gracie was with none of the other women wanting to talk to her and I thought I may as well try to make sure *she* enjoyed the party.' She smiled, lifting an eyebrow. 'We had tea and cupcakes.'

'Then she got stung.' His tone was still flat, but it didn't have the annoyance it had before.

She nodded. 'Then she got stung,' she repeated.

He held her gaze for a moment and it took her almost as long to realise her breaths were shallow, and her chest felt tight. God, it still seemed as though he filled the car more than he actually did. He glanced towards the back of the car, his brow furrowing when he looked back at her.

'You have kids,' he said, almost as though it surprised him.

She frowned. 'I told you that before,' she said.

'I know, I just ... I—' he broke off, snapping his mouth shut. He shifted in his seat to face out through the windscreen.

'I'm not like those other women, Lewis.' She heard the words, but it took her a moment to realise it was her that said them. 'But since I've been unwillingly entered into this ... competition. I am now withdrawing. I'm not looking for anything.'

He let out a groan and her eyes followed where he was looking to see a few of the women starting down the street towards her car, seemingly looking for him. 'I might have misjudged,' he said, looking back at her.

Blue.

And Green.

His eye colour was somewhere between the two, a hint of violet around the edges. A dark colour, not light, though striking all the same. She'd looked at him a few times, and he'd looked at her, but it was the first time she'd noticed how breathtaking his eyes were. And her breath had, indeed, caught in her throat.

'Gracie's my world, you know?' he continued, dropping his gaze. The women were advancing on the car. 'I can't have her being disappointed. That's why I didn't want this, but Mum—she had her own ideas.'

'I get it,' she said, putting the key in the ignition.

The women stopped at the car and peered in. One tapped her knuckles on the window and waved. Lewis held his finger up to them and shifted in his seat to face Brooke again, his brow furrowed. 'What does your husband think about you being here?'

She laughed, feeling her cheeks heat up. Judging by the way he was squinting, he hadn't meant to say *that*. 'Oh, no, I've never been married,' she said, then indicated towards the car seats in the back. 'Brett—their father—and I split when I was pregnant with Ollie.'

He nodded slowly, then smiled. 'Sorry, I—I don't know why I asked that. You wouldn't have been here if you were still with him,'

She smiled. 'I wouldn't have been here at all if I could've avoided it.'

He held her gaze another moment, his lips curved into a slight smile. The women tapped impatiently on the window again and he sighed. 'I don't suppose you could get me out of here?' he said.

She shook her head, her smile broadening, her chest warming. He pressed his lips together, nodding. 'I didn't think so,' he said. 'Well, until next time, then.' He put his hand on the door handle, but hesitated, as though he wanted to say more but wasn't sure if he should.

'Good luck out there,' Brooke said. Anything he might have said would have been pointless since she wasn't after anything at the moment. She wasn't sure if she ever would be. And it seemed he was on the same page as her, even if his mother disagreed. Even if hers disagreed.

He nodded again, opening the door. 'You too,' he said.

He got out of the car and closed the door, moving towards the house with the women talking his ear off. Once he was a few feet away from the car, she felt air suck into her lungs as though she was taking her first breath and realised the car seemed significantly bigger without him in it. And emptier. She watched him walking and gave a little wave as he glanced back at her, but she couldn't help that niggling in her chest. A feeling she couldn't explain. Too bad she'd never see him again.

*Chapter 3*

Brooke gripped the steering wheel tightly, even though the car had stopped moving minutes ago. Her head was all over the place, and she wasn't sure what any of it meant. Her mother had sent her to a match-making party. She had to have known—there was no other excuse for insisting she went to the party. And oh, how it frustrated her. And after being single for only a year and a half!

Being a single working parent was hard enough. What on earth made her mother think she'd have time to develop a relationship with someone? Besides, even if she *did* have time for a relationship, she was sure she was quite capable of finding someone herself. But she didn't have time, and she didn't want to deal with the mess of relationships with young kids.

Even if he had a kid of his own.

It was only setting it up for hearts to be broken—and not just hers. Ollie was too young to know any different, but she still remembered how upset Maddie was when Brett left. He hadn't even had the common decency to still be a part of Maddie's life, save for a phone call on her birthday. He'd never even *met* Ollie.

She took a deep breath and let it out, making sure her exhale made plenty of noise. Then, she climbed out of the car and headed towards her parents' place. She unlocked the door with her spare key and snuck inside, just in case Ollie was asleep. Once she closed the door behind her, Maddie ran past, backtracking when she saw her.

'Mummy!' she yelled, flinging her arms around Brooke's waist. Then, she was off again before Brooke could respond. 'Mummy's back!'

She heard Ollie's squeal from the lounge room and followed the sounds to find him playing with his toys. He rose to his feet when he saw her and toddled over to her. 'Mama! Mama!' he chanted.

She lifted Ollie up and pressed a kiss to his slobbery cheek, shifting him to sit on her hip. He snuggled into her and it made her heart melt. 'Hello, Pops,' she said. Her dad looked up from his book and smiled at her.

'You look nice, sweetheart,' he said. 'Did your mother talk you into going to that party after all?'

'Tricked me, more like it,' she said, teasingly.

'Where is Nan, anyway?'

Since having kids, she'd grown used to calling her parents Nan and Pop around them—just so the kids wouldn't get confused. He flicked his thumb over his shoulder towards the kitchen. She put Ollie back on the ground and headed towards the kitchen. Ollie started crying until her parents' dog, Sugar, ran past him.

'Dog, dog!' he screeched, chasing the Maltese around the couch.

'Hello, *Mother*,' she said emphatically as she reached the kitchen. Maddie squeezed between her and the door with a juice box. She sighed—she was going to have to deal with the hyperactivity later.

Lily looked up from her cookie cutting and frowned. 'You're back early.'

Brooke crossed her arms over her chest. 'Late, in my opinion,' she said, leaning against the bench, and looking down at the cookie dough. Lily was cutting it with a flower-shaped cutter—Maddie's request, she supposed. 'You know, it's a little funny,' she continued. 'There were three guys at the party who weren't part of the catering business—the birthday boy, and I suppose the others were his friends. The rest were all women, and I suspect he didn't know any of them. Would you happen to know anything about that?' She lifted an eyebrow to emphasise her point.

Lily's face tinged pink and she turned away to scuffle in a drawer for something Brooke figured she didn't need.

'*Mother*!'

Lily sighed, turning back towards her. 'Okay, fine, I knew! But can you blame me? You need a nice man and I thought if you two could hit it off—'

'I don't *need* anyone,' Brooke said, rubbing her forehead. 'I'm barely making it through as it is. I don't need to add anything else to my schedule, especially something that takes … time.'

'See, that's where you're wrong,' Lily said, pointing to her with the rolling pin. 'You need some extra help at home and a relationship would provide just that.'

She bit into her lip. 'Relationships are frustrating,' she said. 'And in case you haven't noticed, I *tried* that, with Brett, remember? And you know how that turned out.'

'Oh, Brett is different,' Lily said dismissively. 'He was immature and wasn't ready for a family.' Brooke raised an eyebrow. *She* hadn't been ready for a family either, but they still had one. 'Lewis is already a father,' Lily continued. 'He knows what it's like to be a single parent and he works locally so he'll be home every night.'

Brooke scoffed. 'Seems like you know him better than I do,' she said.

Lily's face tinged again. 'Only from what Gladys has told me. I haven't *met* him, so to speak.' She sighed. 'He's been through so much, I can understand why Gladys wants to see him happy.' She finished rolling out the dough and picked up the cookie cutter. 'And I want to see you happy, too.'

'I *am* happy, Mother,' she said, stealing a chunk from the edge of the rolled-out cookie dough, and popping it in her mouth. 'And I'd imagine he is, too. You've always had Dad, so I don't expect you to understand completely, but it's not just me I have to think about. I can't have the kids getting attached to someone where it doesn't work out.'

'But what if it *does* work out? Honey, you have to understand why I sent you to the party.'

'*That's* another thing,' she said, stealing another chunk of cookie dough. 'If you were so adamant on setting us up, then why didn't you arrange to get us locked in the same elevator or something? What good was it sending me to a party filled with many *beautiful* women in hopes we'd hit it off?'

Lily shrugged, grimacing a little. 'Gladys had already planned the party,' she said. 'I hadn't really thought about the two of you together before then.'

She raised an eyebrow, rolling the chewy cookie dough in her mouth as it stuck to her teeth. 'Well, it was embarrassing,' she said, her words muffled by the dough.

'Did you at least talk to the guy?' Lily said.

'Mhmm,' she mumbled, swallowing as much of the dough as she could. 'But I hadn't planned on it. It kind of ... happened ... when Gracie got stung by a bee.'

'Gracie's his daughter, right?' Lily said. Brooke nodded, using her fingertip to get the remaining dough off the front of her teeth. 'Is she all right?'

'She'll be fine, I'm sure,' she said, tapping her

fingers on the bench. 'I have to go now, to enjoy what's left of my day off. And please, for me, no more meddling. I'm not looking for a relationship. And if I was, I am quite capable of finding one myself.'

Her mother frowned but nodded. Brooke stole another chunk of dough and popped it in her mouth, realising she'd probably taken a piece too big this time. It wouldn't have been the first time.

***

'Thanks for coming!' Lewis said. 'Don't come again,' he added under his breath, a fake smile plastered on his face.

The party was *finally* over, and he was hating the fact *he* was the guest of honour—it meant he couldn't leave until the last guest left. And the last guest who he didn't want there had just walked out the front door. He envied Brooke, being able to leave when she did. He may have asked if she could get him out of there in jest, but he quickly realised he might have been more serious than he realised. Truth is, he hadn't expected for the party to drag on as long as it did. And now, it was almost time for dinner.

'Lewis!' Miles said, drawing out his name. Lewis turned towards the last two of his guests. 'We're going to hit the pub for a few. Are you coming to party on?'

'You need to break the cycle, man, it's been too

long since you've joined us,' Drew added.

He smiled. 'Can't tonight,' he said. 'I've got to get Gracie home.'

He nodded his head towards the little girl curled up on the couch. The party had really taken it out of her. After getting stung, she spent the rest of the afternoon on the couch watching movies. It seems she couldn't last the distance. Truth is, since having Gracie, he'd been forced to grow up. Once he was a single working parent, there was no time to hit the pub. Occasionally, he had his friends over for a few drinks after Gracie had gone to bed. But even *that* hadn't happened for a while.

'Shame,' Drew said. 'Maybe when she's graduated.'

'I'll pencil it in,' he teased. 'Thanks for coming.' He actually meant it with them.

'Wasn't exactly what we were expecting,' Drew said.

'But we got a few numbers,' Miles added, waving his phone between them.

He smiled. He was glad *they*, at least, got something out of it. On the other hand, the only woman he *might* have been interested in left halfway through the party with seemingly no interest in ever seeing him again. He saw his friends out and went in search of his mother. The caterers were making quick work of packing up, and he found Gladys in the kitchen, putting all the leftovers in containers. He rested his elbows on the bench, leaning forward.

'Well, that was embarrassing,' he said.

Gladys scowled at him. 'The amount of effort I put into that party, I'd at least expect some thanks.'

He grinned. 'You *do* realise that ninety percent of those women didn't like the fact I have a kid, right?'

She sighed. 'Well, they were disappointing. What about the other ten percent?'

'I didn't like them.'

'Lewis!'

'What?' he laughed. 'I told you, you shouldn't have meddled.'

She shook her head, smiling. 'There must have been at least *one* you liked.'

There was. But he wouldn't admit who it was. 'Oh, there was *one* woman who seemed all right,' he said. Gladys's eyes lit up. 'And we were both on the same page, would you believe that?'

She smiled broadly. 'Oh, really?'

'Yes,' he said. 'Neither of us are looking for anything.' He spread his arms out in jest. 'Same page.'

'Lewis!' Gladys threw a tea towel at him, scowling.

'Stop meddling, Mother!' he laughed, pulling her into a hug.

He said his goodbyes and gathered Gracie up in his arms. He was happy having one girl in his life, and that girl was snuggling into his chest while he carried her to the car. But he couldn't help but imagine what it would be like to have a mother for Gracie. But her mother was dead. And he couldn't change that. And he couldn't risk it happening again. He wasn't sure he'd be able to go through that again.

He buckled Gracie into her seat and closed the car door, opening the other side's door to put her backpack in when a few more bags appeared next to the backpack. He turned to face his mother.

'Don't want to forget them,' she said. 'There are a few presents, mostly cards. I'm sure you'll probably just toss them all, but please, at least read them before you do.'

He nodded. 'Doesn't change anything, though,' he said.

'A mother can hope,' she said, waving over her shoulder as she walked back to the house.

By the time they got home, Gracie had woken enough to decide she wanted cereal for dinner, a bath, then bed. He obliged, running the bath for her while she ate her cereal. After her bath, he slathered some more honey on the sting—it was already looking better—and redressed her foot with a bandage. Then, he read her a story in bed and tucked her in when she fell asleep halfway through.

It was their usual routine, as he imagined was similar in most houses. He went to the kitchen and made himself a cup of tea, sat down at the table, and stared at the pile of cards and presents in front of him. On one hand, he didn't want to open any of them. What was the point? He probably wouldn't like any of the presents, and what use were cards from people he didn't know?

He sipped his tea, his mind flicking to when he

first saw Brooke at the party, standing next to the table. Somewhere in that pile was a card from her. And it only made him wonder about her sincerity when they talked. If she hadn't wanted to go to the party, why did she have a card? Absently, he picked up the first card on the pile and opened it. Then, the next. Then, the next. One after the other, he opened the cards and skimmed the page. They all said mostly the same things—*Dear Lewis*—followed by a *Happy Birthday* and a brief bio of the card-giver and how they're looking forward to meeting him, ending with a name he'd heard but couldn't put a face to.

Finally, when he was about two-thirds of the way through the pile, he found it. Handwriting that was neat—tall and slanted cursive—and a simple message that, somehow, meant more than anything those other women wrote.

*Dear Lewis,*
*Happy Birthday.*
*Brooke.*

It was so simple it was almost like there was little effort put into it. Her phone number was underneath her name. He put the card down on the table—separately to the pile of other opened cards—and took another sip of tea, staring at the number she'd written. How sincere *was* she, if she was putting her number on the card? Sure, he didn't doubt she was a mother. She knew how to deal with Gracie in a way only a mother could, and she had the car seats in the car to prove it. But the rest of what she said? That she'd been tricked into coming to the party—that she wasn't looking for anything? How much of what she said did he believe?

He put his cup back on the table, one hand still holding onto it while the other reached for his phone. Then, he retracted his hand before he got it. He couldn't contact her. He shouldn't. Already, Gracie seemed more attached to her than he liked. If he ever saw her again, Gracie was likely to get too attached. And he couldn't deal with that. He picked up his tea and took it to bed, picking up the picture frame from his bedside table and staring at the picture of his wedding day.

Alice had been the love of his life. That's what she was supposed to be. There would be no other. That's what he'd promised her when they married. And they'd been happily married for a year before she died. She'd been gone for five years, and the pain could still be just as raw at times. Gracie had taken after her mother, and it made his job harder. She had her big brown eyes, her brown curly hair. He never hid the fact Alice had died from Gracie. He wanted Alice to be as special to Gracie as she had been to him. And he always wanted Gracie to know who her mother was, even if she couldn't *know* her.

He couldn't fall in love again.

Alice had been it for him, he was sure of it. He'd never wanted anyone else. And now, other than having Gracie, he was alone. Heck, he felt guilty if he even *looked* at another woman that way. He didn't want to know how he'd feel if he ever found himself falling for another woman. Or how it would affect

Gracie.

He replaced the frame on the bedside table, next to his tea, and laid back on his bed, staring at the ceiling. The house was quiet—it always had been once Gracie was in bed. But it had never bothered him. It had never felt *too* quiet. Until now. He'd never wanted to succumb to loneliness. Loneliness was a fierce beast he wanted nothing to do with. Unfortunately, it wasn't always that easy.

He closed his eyes and pictured her. Alice. The way her chin-length hair felt between his fingers, her hips beneath his hands. The way her body felt moving against his. He was finding it harder to remember all the details, but he tried his damnedest to hold onto what he could. He knew she had a tiny mole behind one ear—though he couldn't remember which. He'd once enjoyed leaving little kisses on it—a part of her she'd been insecure about. She'd been insecure about many things, but he always tried his best to make sure she wasn't insecure around him.

His mind drifted deeper at the memory of the feel of her thighs tensing against his, the way her breath came heavy, fast. The way she moaned his name as she reached her peak. Though, her voice sounded slightly different. Warmer than her usual softness. He could just about feel her curves as, in his mind, his hands ran up her back to grip her hair but meeting it between her shoulder blades instead of near her chin. It felt wavy, instead of curly, and it was blonde, instead of brown.

And when he saw her face, it wasn't Alice he saw,

but rather the only woman who'd made any kind of lasting impression on him at the party. And she'd done it wearing a blue spaghetti-strapped dress and runners.

# Chapter 4

She felt the weight of his body on hers, the warmth of his breath on her neck that sent a shiver down her spine and her hairs stand on end, awakening each and every one of her senses. She could feel the heat of his lips hovering over her skin, far enough above her to not be touching, close enough to drive her wild with urgency. His body moved against hers in a rhythm that had her wanting more. Her hands ran across the planes of his back, her fingertips digging into his shoulders as he pushed her closer to the edge. She felt the sensational trail he left from the hollow of her neck to her chin, nipping, sucking, until his lips hovered just above hers, teasing her, his breath mingling with hers. He looked at her with an intensity she'd never known, his blue-green eyes darkening with desire, and she could feel her heart quickening, her breaths coming heavier, until—

'Mum.'

Brooke looked into Maddie's round blue eyes, the memories of her dream still lingering at the back of her mind and took a deep breath—an attempt to control her quickened breathing and to shake the thoughts from her mind.

'Morning, sweetheart,' she said, her voice croaky.

'Ollie's awake,' Maddie said, throwing herself on Brooke for a quick cuddle.

The fuzz in Brooke's head started to clear and she could hear Ollie mumbling from their room. She nodded as Maddie slid off the bed and bounced towards the door. She tried to prop herself up on her elbows, then collapsed back against the bed. 'I'll be out in a minute,' she mumbled.

She heard the patter of Maddie's feet move down the hallway and Ollie's squeals. Brooke smiled. Maddie had always been a good helper with Ollie, and Ollie adored his big sister. Going from the squeals of delight she could hear, she figured Maddie had bought her a few more minutes.

She blinked up at the ceiling, trying to ease herself awake, trying to think of things a little less … sensual … than her dream. *Her dream*. She hadn't had a sex dream before. Not even about Brett. In fact, she rarely dreamed. The closest she'd ever had to a sex dream was that one time when some guy she'd seen on a poster advertising men's briefs showed up in a dream and offered her a slice of pizza. That was about as sexy as her dreams got.

Until now.

A dream like that about a guy she barely knew—who she hadn't even touched before—was more confusing than anything. And entirely unwanted. Well, not *completely*. She'd be lying if she said she didn't enjoy it. She groaned, closing her eyes, feeling flustered.

It had been three full days since she'd met Lewis—today would be the fourth—and she hadn't been able to get him out of her mind when she was awake. And now, he'd made his way into her unconscious self's mind, too. It had taken her thoughts to a whole other level. She felt both ... ashamed ... and a little bit ... curious. The dream had been so realistic—so much so, she half-expected him to be in her bed with her when she woke up. She was a little disappointed he wasn't.

She felt her cheeks heat up and banished the thought. She'd told her mother—and him—that she wasn't looking for anything. She was happy with how her life is. She was busy enough already. Adding a relationship on top of that would just make things ... complicated. Heck, simply surviving the day was a battle most of the time. She had no time or effort leftover to put into a relationship, and she'd managed to keep busy enough to ignore the loneliness.

But not even keeping herself busy at work could get her mind off him—she imagined busying herself with the kids on her day off would do just as little.

She sighed, rolling herself up to sit on the side of the bed. It wouldn't work. Not with him, not with anyone. Maybe, when the kids were older—*much* older—she might find herself with some extra time. But in the near, foreseeable future, relationships were out of the question for her. She just had to keep making it through a day at a time.

Still, it didn't stop her mind from wondering how it *would* feel with Lewis. If her dream was anything to go by, it would be good. *Really* good. But she knew how it was with Brett, and it was *nothing* like her dream. She reminded herself it's called fantasy for a reason. Wishing it could ever be a reality would just be a waste of time and breath.

She let out another forceful sigh, coming to a logical decision. What were the chances of ever seeing him again, anyway? She'd lived in Bendigo her whole life and never once met him before. She was certain she was likely to never see him again—at least, not for a long time. It made sense their paths might cross sometime in the very, very distant future, but in the meantime, chances were very slim. And she had no way to contact him, and he had no way to contact her. She might not be able to get him out of her mind for now, but soon enough, she'd stop thinking about him.

For now, she already had a busy enough day lined up. Going to the shops with the kids was like giving them a litre of red cordial, then trying to stop them from bouncing off the walls. It was almost guaranteed to stop her thinking about Lewis. At least for a little while.

***

It didn't.

Not even for a second.

Not when she had to keep both kids under control and stop Ollie from running away from her when he refused to be in his stroller. Not when Maddie picked up just about every single thing they passed and begged for it, whining when Brooke said she couldn't have it. Not when Ollie snuck a bunch of toys into the mesh basket underneath the stroller without her realising, resulting in a thorough check through all of her bags and threats from security, despite her efforts at trying to explain the situation.

Not when she *finally* managed to get Ollie to sleep in the stroller and certainly not when she had to bribe Maddie with treats to be good. And it was *impossible* to not think about him when she practically bumped into him in her desperation for food and coffee and somewhere to sit down. And she knew it would be an incredibly long time before she would forget about him when his eyes connected with hers.

***

Surprisingly, it didn't take him long to recognise her, despite the fact he'd only ever seen her once before in a blue spaghetti-strapped dress. And every night since then in his dreams. He recognised her eyes first—the rich honey colour was brighter today—then her hair, pulled into the same ponytail she'd had at the party. She had both kids with her, it seemed. Ollie—he assumed—was asleep in the stroller, and Maddie was holding onto the handle of the stroller. She looked as though she had them under control, but also seemed to have a sense of urgency about her. He felt a tug on his arm and looked down at Gracie—a wide smile on her face and just about bouncing with excitement. *Shoot.*

'Look, Daddy! It's Brooke!'

She tugged her hand free of his grip and practically launched herself towards Brooke, wrapping her arms around her waist. He felt a fist clench in his chest. He'd thought he'd never see Brooke again. He'd decided it was probably for the best. That's why he'd spent every last bit of energy he had busying himself, so he wouldn't call her. He tried to forget about her. But he couldn't. He figured he would with time. But how could he, now?

Brooke's face reddened as she patted Gracie softly on her back, then she seemed to recover quickly, bending down between the two girls. 'Hi, Gracie,' she said. 'Remember me telling you about Maddie?' Gracie nodded. 'This is her,' Brooke said, pulling Maddie closer. 'Maddie, this is Gracie.'

The two girls mumbled hellos and looked shyly at the ground. Brooke straightened, smiling at him. He felt his heartbeat quicken and shook the thoughts from his mind. Why should he feel guilty about simply bumping into her at the shops? It's not as though it was planned.

'Morning,' she said.

He felt his lips twitch in a smile. 'Afternoon.'

Her cheeks reddened again, and she glanced down at her watch. Then, she laughed. 'So it is,' she said. 'It's funny because it hasn't really been morning for hours. I suppose I lost track of time.'

He nodded, glancing down at Gracie and Maddie who had started talking. Gracie was showing Maddie her new bracelet—her spoils of the day. 'Same here,' he said, glancing back up at her. He held out the kebab in his hand, still hot in its packet. 'We were just about to have lunch. Do you want ... to ... join us?'

He squinted, wondering what compelled him to say that. Maybe it was because their children seemed to be getting along, and if they were busy talking to each other, it gave him and Brooke a chance to catch their breath. Taking Gracie to the shops was a big enough task for him—with all the touching things and the rushing off. He had to bribe her with whatever she wanted for lunch to get her to stop running off on him. Brooke was doing it with two kids. He wondered if she had to use bribery, too. He glanced back down at the girls. They were now holding hands, Maddie tugging on Brooke's arm.

'Mum, can we go play on that?' she said, pointing to the kids play area at the end of the food court. 'Oh, *please*!' She drew out the syllables.

Brooke hummed, looking up at him questioningly.

He glanced around the food court. Being after the normal lunch rush, it wasn't too busy. And there were a few tables free near the play area. He waved the kebab again, smiling. How much harm could having lunch together in a food court do? Brooke sighed, focussing back on the girls.

'All right,' she said. The girls jumped excitedly and started running off towards the play area. 'But stay where I can see you!' she called after them. She focussed back on him, letting out another visible sigh. 'I suppose we'll be joining you, after all.'

'Great,' he said, feeling cheesy that his grin was wider than it should be. 'I was just about to get some coffee, want some?'

Her eyes widened, and her shoulders seemed to relax. She almost looked … relieved. 'I'd *love* one,' she said, pulling her purse out of the back of the stroller. 'Can I—'

'My shout,' he said, surprising himself. 'Gracie wants a muffin for lunch, would Maddie like one?'

Brooke smiled, her eyes shining. 'It's about all she'll eat,' she said.

'We're *very* healthy,' he said sarcastically, shifting closer to her to let someone pass.

She laughed again, making the fist clench tighter in his chest, and making his smile widen. A mixed feeling he couldn't quite define. 'I'm so over looking for something *healthy* that they'll eat,' she said, her eyes dancing. 'As long as they're fed, I don't really care what they eat half the time.'

'Muffins it is, then,' he said. He pointed towards

Ollie, who was still asleep. 'Anything for him?'

She grabbed a baby food pouch from the stroller and held it up. 'He's sorted.'

He laughed, remembering how those pouches practically saved his life when Gracie was a baby. He had always liked cooking, but when Gracie had flat out refused all the meals he made, he didn't know what else to do. She basically spent the first two years of her life living off cereal, bananas, and those pouches until she grew to like his food.

He held the kebab out towards her. 'Kebab?'

'Oh, no, that's yours,' she said.

He shrugged. 'I'll get another.' He gave the kebab a jiggle. 'It's chicken.'

Her eyebrow lifted. 'Salads?'

'Everything. Waste of money, otherwise.'

Her lips curved up. 'Sauce?'

'Barbecue,' he said, jiggling it again. 'You know you want it.'

She sighed. 'It *is* how I have it.'

'Well, you take this one,' he said, indicating to the tables near the play area. 'And sit down somewhere over there, and I'll be back with some liquid gold.'

She laughed, and it made his stomach flip. *Liquid gold*? It hadn't been the first time he'd used those words to describe coffee, but it still sounded a little corny saying it now. She took the kebab from his outstretched hand, her fingers brushing against his, sending a spark shooting up his arm.

'This all adds up, though,' she said. 'Are you sure I can't give you anything towards it?'

He shook his head, moving back into the kebab line. 'I've got it this time,' he teased. 'If it makes you feel better, you can get it next time.'

She seemed to consider him for a moment, then smiled. A beautiful smile that almost stunned him. The way her lips curved up—slightly higher on the left side—the way her eyes looked as though they were dancing. She dropped her gaze, pressing her lips together as if trying to hide the smile but only succeeding in making her look cuter.

'Thank you, Lewis,' she said softly. 'I might just take you up on that offer.'

He smiled back, watching as she manoeuvred the stroller between the tables towards the play area. He didn't know why he mentioned a next time. And he felt as though he was liking the idea of it a hell of a lot more than he should. Why shouldn't he see her again? Even if neither of them were looking for something, there was no harm in being friends, at least. After all, it seemed both of their girls had hit it off rather quickly, and he always hoped Gracie was making friends.

Sure, she'd told him about other kids at kindergarten being her friends, but he'd honestly never seen himself as the kind of guy to do playdates. It just never really appealed to him, being a single father. Especially since he was fairly certain that most, if not all, of those playdates would be with the child's mother—probably mostly partnered. Not to mention the fact he never really had much time outside of work and preferred to spend the bit of time he did have with his daughter.

But Brooke?

She was in the same situation as him, and they were both on the same page. There was nothing stopping a friendship from forming. And judging by the way Gracie and Maddie were becoming fast friends, they were more than likely going to be forced into arranging playdates for the kids. Forced, because he knew Gracie would not stop begging for another chance to play with Maddie after this.

The only thing that could come between them at least being friends was the fact his body betrayed him around her. And from only being this close to her twice, that was something that concerned him. But he also knew if he never contacted her again after this, it would probably be the biggest regret he ever had.

Partly because Gracie would drive him to the brink of insanity.

Mostly because his thoughts and his dreams would push him over it.

He was screwed either way. *Damn.*

***

Brooke took a shallow breath, rocking the stroller gently to ease Ollie back into sleep. She thought she'd never see Lewis again. And here she was, about to have lunch with the guy—of which he was paying for—in a food court in the middle of a busy shopping centre. She did not see that coming.

She also didn't expect her stomach to start feeling like it was going to explode into a million butterflies, or her desperate-for-food-and-coffee brain fuzz to become a full-fledged inability to think clearly. She could have got out of it. She only had to make up something about having to leave. Plans for the rest of the afternoon. *Anything* that would mean she didn't have to have lunch with the guy she'd had a sex dream about last night.

She'd felt her cheeks heat up the second he caught her eye, and images of his body moving against hers, his kisses—it was so vivid she could have sworn his lips lingered where they'd touched in her dream—made her feel flushed. How the hell could she have *lunch* with him after that?

She took a few more quick breaths, followed by a slow, deep one in an attempt to compose herself. Why hadn't she refused his offer to have lunch with him? Because she was focussed on food and coffee, for starters. Because he caught her by surprise. Because she desperately needed to sit down and feel like she wasn't struggling with the kids for once. Because she felt for Gracie. And she yearned for Maddie to have a friend who she already knew was sweet.

She wasn't into having playdates with other kids from Maddie's kindergarten, and she didn't have any other mum friends. And seeing how easily the two girls were getting along, it made her happy. She just wasn't sure how she could sustain that kind of friendship with Lewis. Especially if she was having sex

                    *R.J. Groves*

dreams about him.

But this was only lunch. In a food court. And although it wasn't exactly busy at the moment, there were still people around. She took another deep breath, finally feeling like she had everything under control. At least for now. And just in time for Lewis to return to the table with the food, a visual reminder he'd mentioned a next time, making the nervousness return in her stomach.

He might have said she could pay for it next time to get her to accept the fact he was paying for it today. But he could have actually meant it, too. Was that his way of ensuring there would be a next time? If so, it was clever on his behalf, but she still didn't know exactly how she felt about it. Perhaps it was entirely innocent, and she was reading *way* too far into it. Maybe he was simply referring to a future playdate for the kids, or just covering his bases if they ever bumped into each other at the shops again.

She just had to convince her body it was entirely innocent, which it was convinced it wasn't, considering he sat in the seat next to her. But it made sense if she thought about it. Where he sat ensured both of them could keep an eye on Maddie and Gracie. It was a logical spot to sit. Even if it meant his knee might rest against hers, making her very aware of his closeness. Her body felt like it was vibrating, even though she wasn't shaking.

Maybe it was just for now—a temporary adjustment to being so close to a man again. It had been a while, after all. She hadn't had so much as coffee with an eligible guy since she and Brett separated. It had just never been a priority. And it still wasn't, as far as she was concerned. But there was something about Lewis that made even the idea of coffee not seem as innocent as it was supposed to be.

'I got a milkshake for Maddie,' he said, unloading the tray of drinks and food. 'I hope that's okay. I forgot to ask, and only remembered Gracie wanted one when I was over there.'

He finished unloading the tray and leaned back in his chair, putting it on the table behind them that was empty except for the dirty dishes left from the last people sitting there.

'Thanks,' she mumbled, surprised at his thoughtfulness. 'What flavour?'

'Strawberry,' he said, picking up one of the kebabs from the table—the one he first got, she noticed—and started peeling the wrapping back. 'All little girls like strawberry, right? It's pink.'

She smiled. 'You'll probably be her new favourite person, then,' she said, picking up the fresher kebab. She had a feeling he hadn't picked up the first kebab by accident, and it spread a warmth through her stomach.

He smiled back, biting into his kebab. 'You know,' he said, only a little muffled from the food. 'You didn't have to wait for me to get back to start eating.'

She shrugged. 'I didn't want to be finished by the

time you got back.'

His eyebrow lifted, and she felt her cheeks heat up. 'You eat that fast?' he said, his eyes teasing.

'I'm a mother,' she said, taking a big bite, and regretting it instantly. How was she to know how to act appropriately around a guy? How could she know what was etiquette and what wasn't? She couldn't even remember the last time she'd been able to enjoy a meal slowly, uninterrupted. Without having to share with anyone. 'I have to,' she added, though she was sure he could barely make out the words.

His lips curved upwards, a smile that made his eyes seem brighter. 'You don't have to now, though,' he said, nodding his head towards the kids, then the stroller. 'They're preoccupied and he's as—'

'Don't say it!' she said, slapping her hand over her mouth so she wouldn't spray food everywhere.

He laughed, his expression amused. 'You don't believe in jinxes, do you?'

'No,' she grumbled, sipping her coffee now she'd finished that bite. 'But I do know kids have a terrible habit of doing the opposite of what you say. Like if you say they finally s-l-e-e-p through the night, or they e-a-t anything. Suddenly, they don't anymore.'

'I have *never* had that problem,' he said, his eyes dancing. He took another mouthful of his kebab.

'Well *you* are a guy,' she said, taking a smaller bite.

'Maybe I've just been lucky enough to have a kid that always slept well.'

'Why would you say that?'

'What?'

'The s-word,' she whispered.

'Sleep?'

'You did it again! You know, I spelled it out for a reason.' She shot her eyes towards the stroller, holding her breath.

He laughed. 'I wondered why you did that,' he said. 'I thought you were just being superstitious.'

She nodded her head towards Ollie. His eyes were wide, and his lip quivered once he saw her food. 'Is *that* being superstitious?' She took a chunk of chicken small enough for Ollie from her kebab and popped it in his mouth.

'Hmm,' Lewis said, rolling another mouthful around in his mouth. 'That could just be a coincidence.'

She felt her eyebrow lift, amused, and pointed to the muffins. 'I'd spell those out, too, if I were you.'

His brow furrowed. 'What, muffins?'

As if on cue, Ollie spat the chicken out of his mouth and started crying. She squinted at Lewis. 'I hate you.'

Lewis tilted his head, considering her for a moment. 'You don't mean that.'

'I might.'

'So, he knows what muffins are, that doesn't mean I have to spell it out.'

Ollie's crying escalated, and Brooke took him out of the stroller, sitting him on her lap. 'You just don't learn, do you?' she teased. 'The whole point of spelling is to avoid *this*.'

'So, should I spell milkshake, too?'

She lifted an eyebrow. 'I would have.'

He opened his mouth to say something but was interrupted by Maddie and Gracie swarming to the table, plonking themselves on the other seats at the table and pulling the muffins closer. Gracie reached for one of the milkshakes.

'Is this mine, Daddy?'

Lewis pressed his lips together in amusement, nodding his head slowly. 'Yes, it is,' he said. 'And the other is for Maddie.' He turned his head back to face Brooke. She smirked, knowing her point couldn't have been proven any better. 'All right, point taken.'

'Mummy, why's Ollie crying?' Maddie said, crumbs falling out of her full mouth. It seemed she must have got that habit from Brooke.

'Because he wants a muffin, too,' she said, jigging him on her lap as his crying turned into a borderline tantrum.

'He can have some of mine,' Gracie said, nudging her muffin closer.

'And mine,' Maddie added.

Brooke smiled, thanking the girls as they parted with some of their muffins and she glanced up at an amused expression on Lewis's face.

'I thought you had food for him,' he said.

She feigned a look of shock. 'Do you really think he'll eat that when there are *muffins* available?'

He laughed, holding her gaze, and it made her stomach flip. Stupid stomach. Their conversation seemed to come naturally, even if they did spend a good portion of it arguing about the usefulness of spelling around kids. She felt like she had him converted in the end, but she couldn't be too sure. What she *was* certain of, though, was that he was most likely to make more appearances in her dreams.

Stupid dreams.

# *Chapter 5*

He thought it was weird, at first. Then, it was cute. He'd never heard of someone having those kinds of opinions with kids. Then again, he hadn't exactly been in many conversations with other parents. Maybe it was a mother thing. Either way, before now, spelling words around your kids so they don't go nuts never occurred to him. But now, after seeing how everything unfolded at the table while he refused to spell the words, he was convinced it had its benefits.

He accredited his lack of spelling knowledge to the fact it was just him and Gracie at home, always had been since Gracie was born. Clearly, Brooke had hung around with someone long enough to have a second child. It didn't surprise him she had more spelling experience around kids than he did.

They'd moved from the table to the play area, him and Brooke leaning against the fence while the kids played. They were the only ones playing on the equipment, and they figured Ollie could play, too, if they were there with them. Partly because it seemed Ollie didn't want to be too far away from Brooke. He could tell it must be exhausting for her, and he'd heard boys could be clingy when they're babies. He couldn't speak from experience, though.

Gracie had always been a fairly independent child, and it wouldn't surprise him if Maddie was, too. The two girls seemed to be alike in many ways and were playing together like they'd been best friends for years. Brooke put Ollie on the ground in another attempt at getting him to play, but he clung to her legs, sobbing.

'Is he always like that?' he asked, hoping it didn't come out wrong.

Brooke nodded. 'He's a clingy bub,' she said, sighing. 'Which is kind of sweet, in a way, but incredibly exhausting. How was Gracie?'

'Independent from the start,' he said. 'Maddie?'

She nodded. 'Independent,' she leaned back against the fence of the play area, seemingly relieved as Ollie stopped sobbing to watch the girls playing. He was still clinging to her legs, though. 'I wonder if it's a dad thing,' she continued, folding her arms across her chest.

She looked weary, and he wondered how much trouble the kids put her through. He knew Gracie kept him on his toes. He figured Maddie was probably similar to Gracie, but she also had to deal with a clingy one-year-old.

'I mean,' she said. 'Gracie has you around and she's independent. Maddie had her dad around for the first few years, and she's independent. Ollie's only had me, and he's clingy.'

'Maybe it's just a kid thing,' he said, shrugging. 'Maybe girls are just naturally independent, and boys are clingy.'

She smiled. 'That would probably make more sense,' she said. 'But I'm only really going off what we've experienced with these kids. I don't really … talk … to other mums.'

'Neither do I,' he said. 'I mean, she has friends at kindergarten, but I just don't talk to their parents.'

'Right?' she said, looking at him with her honey-coloured eyes. The colour seemed to warm since they'd been talking. 'Talking to them is overrated. I mean, if they end up in the same school, then I *might* talk to them. One day. But I'm not sure I could deal with that right now.'

'Or ever,' he teased.

She laughed, her head slightly tilted towards the ground, her fringe falling over her eyes. He fought the urge to tuck it behind her ear. No, he couldn't touch her. He was sure he wouldn't be able to keep to any friendship if he did. He'd be more focussed on how her cheek felt beneath his thumb, and whether or not her hair felt the same way he'd imagined it would sliding between his fingers. He dropped his gaze, worried he wouldn't be able to control himself if he even *looked* at her for longer than he should.

Who was this woman?

They seemed to have a whole lot more in common than he'd first thought. She seemed real, down to earth, able to laugh about the weirdest of things, like spelling out words in front of kids, or not wanting to talk to other parents. The total opposite of what any of those other women at the party were. She'd said she wasn't looking for anything, and neither was he. But it seemed as though they were at least going to be pulled into having playdates if the girls had anything to say about it.

'Or ever,' she repeated softly, watching as Ollie finally let go of her leg and toddled after the girls. 'It's not that I'm anti-social,' she added. 'I guess I just don't have … time … to deal with playdates all the time. I suppose you feel the same.' She glanced up at him, and he nodded, unsure exactly of what she was saying. She dropped her gaze again. 'I mean, playdates with one person are one thing, but having to organise them with like … five … other people is ridiculous. I don't know how some people do it.'

'I guess some people have nothing else going on,' he offered.

'Like work.'

'Like work,' he repeated, nodding.

'I only get two days off a week, you know,' she said. 'Wednesdays and Saturdays. And when you don't get more than one day off in a row, it's hard to try to fit in catching up with lots of people.'

'I could imagine.'

'When do you work?' she looked back up at him, her eyes questioning.

He shrugged. 'Weekdays. I'm a building contractor, so I get most weekends off.'

Her brow furrowed. 'But it's Wednesday. You're not working today?'

'We sometimes get a day off between projects if we finish earlier than expected.'

She nodded slowly. 'That's a good incentive.'

'It is,' he agreed. 'It's a good boost for morale, too. Where do you work?'

'*McEwen's Jewellers*,' she said, her eyebrow lifting. 'I get no such incentive.'

*McEwen's Jewellers*. If he recalled correctly, that was on the main street of town, a few doors up from the café they often frequented. At his work, being a smaller, close-knit workplace, they had a sort of rotating system where they'd all take turns in getting coffee for everyone—once in the morning at the start of the workday, and again in the afternoon to get them through the last couple of hours.

'And you don't get Sundays off?' he said. 'I would have thought you'd get the whole weekend off, at least, since you have kids.'

She scoffed. 'I'm lucky to even *have* the job *because* I have kids,' she said. 'I mean, it would be a problem if I had them in childcare, but my parents help out a lot, so I don't have to.'

He nodded. 'Mum's the same,' he said. 'She helped a lot when Gracie was a baby, so it just made sense to continue with it. She'll be in school next year, though. I don't know what Mum will do with all her spare time.'

He held her gaze, her dancing eyes making him smile. He thought he could see something there, something in the way she looked at him, though he couldn't quite work it out. But in the way her eyes danced, and their colour hit a shade warmer than they were before, it stirred something inside him. An urge he shouldn't act on. Her fringe still fell over the corner of her eye and he found himself fighting the urge to tuck it behind her ear again. And he was about to give in to that urge when she did it herself, diverting her gaze towards the kids. He followed suit, seeing the two girls walking with Ollie between them, holding his hands.

Why couldn't friendships be as simple as that? At what stage did being friends with someone be so much harder than it ever was when he was a kid? As a kid, life is simple, there's nothing *really* to be worried about, even when you haven't been dealt the best life. Kids make the most of it.

'Umm ... Gracie's mother,' Brooke said hesitantly. 'You never said what happened to her.' He focussed back on her. She'd dropped her gaze to the floor, her arms folded across her chest. She took a deep breath—he could tell by the rise and fall of her chest. 'I mean, you don't *have* to tell me if you don't want to. I get it. I just ... I—'

She snapped her mouth shut and swallowed. He waited a moment, to see if she was going to finish

                    *R.J. Groves*

her sentence. But when she said nothing, he rubbed his forehead.

'She died,' he said simply.

He couldn't even say the word for the first few years, let alone talk about it. But then he realised that it was how it was. Nothing was going to bring her back, and the longer he went without being able to say the words, the longer it would take for him to heal. He was sure he would never truly get over the fact his wife had been taken from him too soon. But he could at least be able to cope better. Even if he could never really move on.

Brooke's eyes shot up towards him, glistening, this time, instead of dancing. 'God, I'm so sorry,' she whispered.

He fought the urge to smooth out the crease on her forehead, dropping his gaze to make sure he kept his hands to himself. 'It's not your fault,' he said, shrugging. He didn't want to be pitied. He'd worked hard to make sure Gracie had a life she could be proud of. Pity had no place in that.

'Still,' she said. He felt her fingertips touch his arm, and when he looked up at her, realised she'd shifted to face him. Shifted closer. He could feel the pulsing in his arm where she touched him, a pulsing that lingered, even after she'd retracted her hand. 'How did she ...'

She spoke softly, laced with concern. He took a shaky breath. 'Alice ... umm ... she got caught in a car accident when she was seven months pregnant.'

Brooke's hand shot up to cover her mouth, her

eyes glistening more than they were before, though she had yet to shed a tear. He looked towards the kids, worried if he held her gaze, he might not tell her at all.

'With Gracie,' he continued. 'She was critical when they took her to the hospital, but she held on. They said the few words she said when she kept dropping in and out of consciousness were *my baby, save my baby*.' He rubbed his eyes, taking a moment to catch his breath, steady his voice. 'It's as though she knew she was going to die.'

'God, Lewis,' she whispered.

He nodded slowly. 'They could see it, too,' he said. 'They took her straight into an emergency caesarean and lost her before Gracie could be born.'

'But Gracie was okay.'

'Gracie had to be resuscitated and spent a month in an incubator, and another two weeks in the nursery until she was ready to come home. I almost lost her, too.'

***

Brooke could barely keep herself together. She swallowed the lump in her throat, doing her best to hold back the tears. She couldn't even imagine what Lewis went through. Just hearing him talk about it made her heart ache, made her want to reach out to him and, somehow, erase the pain he would have felt—that he probably still had. She'd had easy pregnancies. Full-term. No complications.

But she'd been absolutely terrified of SIDS. She remembered the anxiety she felt after her kids were born. Checking on them repeatedly while they slept, unable to catch sleep herself. She'd been more worried about Maddie—she'd always slept well, and even had to be woken for feedings. But Ollie, though he was still yet to have a night where he slept through, was no exception. She knew she wouldn't have been able to function right if she'd lost either of them. And at one stage, she might have felt the same about Brett.

At least with Brett, there had been a long lead-up to him leaving. And leaving was very different from dying. Even if he couldn't be bothered to keep in contact for his kids' sakes.

'I had no idea,' she whispered. 'It must have been so hard for you.'

He nodded, and when he looked up at her, his eyes were dark. She could tell it still filled him with sadness, even if it happened five years ago. 'It was,' he said. 'I never left Gracie's side for the first few days, you know.'

She nodded. She could understand why he wouldn't have. He was scared to lose her too, she supposed. And he didn't want to let her out of his sight like Alice had been. She wondered if he ever blamed himself for losing her. He shouldn't. It wasn't his fault. But she knew she would have blamed herself if she was in the same kind of situation. It's just the way it worked.

'The nurses kept telling me she would be okay,

that I didn't have to be there every second of every day. But she was all I had. I didn't want to go home. If I went home, I would be reminded of Alice. I could put it off just that little bit longer if I stayed at the hospital with Gracie.'

Brooke swallowed. If she was in his shoes, she would have been the same. She supposed a lot of people would have been. Going home to an empty house, knowing the person you cared for most would never be returning. It would be a difficult task. She remembered feeling shocked when Brett left, even though she knew it was coming. She couldn't imagine how Lewis would have felt when he came home one day knowing things were very different. And he couldn't change it.

'Was Gracie a name she picked out?' she asked hesitantly.

He smiled, his eyes growing lighter. 'We hadn't agreed on a name, no. Gracie wasn't even in the shortlisted names. But when she was born, none of those other names seemed to suit her. And I figured it was only with grace she survived, so Gracie seemed very fitting.'

She swiped at her eyes, relieved she hadn't turned into a bawling fit—sad stories almost always made her cry, especially if she could relate in any way, or had any kind of personal tie with whoever was going through it. Her heart ached for Gracie. Maddie and Ollie only had to deal with their father not being around. They might know him one day, they might even have a relationship with him. But

Gracie never even got a chance to meet her mother, and never will. She was so lucky she had a father as strong and incredible as Lewis was.

'It suits her so well,' she said, her voice cracking slightly.

'I thought so,' he said, his eyes flashing. He cleared his throat, glancing over at the kids. 'We should probably head off.'

'Oh … of course … me too,' she stammered, unsure of why she felt disappointed.

'Where are you parked?'

'Under the shades,' she said, lifting her eyebrow.

He smiled. 'Same. We'll walk with you.'

Her heart skipped a beat, despite being disappointed their impromptu playdate had come to an end. They gathered up the kids and started heading out towards the cars. She'd put Ollie back in the stroller, and Maddie and Gracie were walking hand in hand next to her. Lewis was on her other side, his shoulder occasionally bumping into hers, sending a shiver down her spine.

'Your kids,' he said as they walked. 'Their dad—is he still around?'

She lifted an eyebrow, looking up at him. There was something in the way he tried to keep a straight face, something in the way he asked the question, that made her wonder why he was asking. Sure, she'd asked about Gracie's mother, but it was just in the way he asked the question that made her wonder. Unless she was reading *way* too much into it, it seemed as though he was trying to scope out the situation. Or, it could be completely innocent. Like all of this probably is.

She shook her head. 'He left when I was pregnant with Ollie,' she said. 'We haven't seen him since. He's called Maddie a couple times. Birthdays, that kind of thing. But that's it.'

Lewis blew out some air, shaking his head slowly. 'Obviously, there'd be a reason why it didn't work out with you two. I get that. But to not want to be involved with his kids? I couldn't imagine not being able to see my kids—Gracie. Not being able to see … Gracie.' He glanced towards her, catching her eye for a moment before looking out around the carpark.

Her brow furrowed, and she tilted her head to the side, stopping at the back of her car. He looked at her questioningly. *Had* he had an ulterior motive with his question? She took a shaky breath. 'Brett's not much of a … family … man,' she said slowly. 'He worked in the mines. Fly in, fly out, that kind of thing. He was away a lot, and it suited him.'

'But not you?' he asked hesitantly.

She shook her head. 'I couldn't rely on him,' she continued. 'He'd sometimes skip his home time— taking on more work, I thought. But I never saw the money from it. I—' she sighed. 'I don't really know what he was doing in that time. But he wouldn't bother to tell me he wouldn't be home until I'd already started freaking out, wondering where he was.'

She thought she saw Lewis's jaw clench, but he didn't say anything. She wondered what was going

                    *R.J. Groves*

through his mind, what he was thinking about. Going from what she could see of him with Gracie, Lewis was a family man. He wouldn't be the kind of guy to not bother with telling his woman he'd be late home. She imagined he would more likely be the kind of guy to ring when he was on his way home. Or maybe she hoped he would be, despite her efforts at trying not to grow fond of him. She had to keep him at arm's length. She had to stop her mind from going there— dwelling on thoughts of what it would be like with him, what his lips felt like against hers. His body.

She cleared her throat, fiddling with a bit of loose foam on the stroller handle. Maddie and Gracie were both leaning against the car, whispering to each other—another reminder why she couldn't get too attached to Lewis. It was just the fact she hadn't spent this kind of time with a guy since Brett, she was sure of it. And even when she was with Brett, they hadn't *really* spent that much time together. She couldn't even remember when she'd had a guy giving her any kind of attention like this.

'That was one of the reasons why it didn't work, anyway,' she muttered. 'He also came back from work with chlamydia one time. I think that was the last straw.' She bit into her lip, wondering if she'd told him too much. She glanced up at him, his eyes were wide, his brow furrowed, his jaw seemingly tenser than before.

'He *cheated* on you?' His voice was deep, raw. Almost a growl. Briefly, she thought that Brett was probably lucky he wasn't still hanging around.

She shrugged, pushing a smile onto her face. 'I guess the grub thought I wouldn't find out.'

Lewis's expression softened, and though he still looked tense, his lips curved into a slight smile, his eyebrow lifting. 'Grub?'

Her smile widened. 'Well, I'm not going to call him a b-a-s-t-a-r-d in front of the kids, am I?'

He seemed to relax, his smile matching hers. 'I'm not sure calling him a g-r-u-b is much better,' he teased.

She scoffed. 'There is nothing wrong with grub,' she said. 'If there's something you should know about me, it's that I will use that word a lot. And dag.' He lifted an eyebrow, his expression amused. She felt her cheeks heat up and busied herself with getting the bags off the stroller. 'It's an endearing term!'

'Oh, I *know* what a dag is, Brooke,' he teased. 'And I would not exactly call it endearing.'

She popped the boot open, loading the bags into it. 'It has many uses, *Lewis*. And one of them is as an endearing term. Look it up.'

'Maybe I will,' he said his eyebrow lifting.

She smiled at him, holding his gaze for a simple moment. A moment too long that ended too soon, in her opinion. She felt her breath catch in her throat, wondering what was going through his head. Confused at what was going through her head. She was usually an awkward person. Sure, she talked to customers, and she was confident in doing that. But she was slow to make friends, hesitant. She rarely gave away much about herself so quickly. But that all seemed to be thrown out the window with Lewis.

In the short time she'd known him, he'd already managed to get her to tell him why her last relationship didn't work, where and when she works, her kebab order, the fact her kids practically lived off cereal and muffins half the time, *and* she used some strange … *endearing* … terms. Hell, he'd even met her kids. He directed his gaze to her car, his brow furrowed.

'You're here?'

She frowned. Why else did he think she'd stopped? She nodded. 'Didn't you recognise the car?'

He groaned, leaning his head back to stare up at the shades above them. 'I know I *should*, being a guy and all,' he said, laughing. He looked at the car next to hers—a white ute that looked as though it'd seen a lot of work. 'But I'm really not very good with the models or anything like that.' He looked back at her, indicating with his head towards the ute. 'I actually thought you somehow knew what *my* car looked like and that's why you stopped.'

His eyes were dancing, his smile flashing his straight white teeth, somehow making her stomach flip again. He hadn't noticed he'd parked next to her? She knew he'd parked next to her and not the other way around because there hadn't been a car on that side of her's when she parked there. She took a deep breath, trying to calm her flipping stomach, and her stupid nerves, and that weird, funny feeling that had niggled at her insides since she bumped into him at the food court. Brett would have recognised her car. He was able to recognise it a mile away, which confused her since he was rarely home to see it. Then again, he *had* been a little … protective … controlling … when they were together.

Gracie tugged on his arm and he crouched down to her level. 'Daddy, can we have a playdate with Maddie? *Please*?'

Lewis looked up at Brooke, his eyebrow lifted, his eyes questioning. She bit into her lip. How much harm could it be? Obviously, they got along well enough to have a conversation. An enjoyable one, at that. And it wasn't as embarrassing as she'd thought it would be, considering her dream. And the girls had made fast friends. *Very* fast friends. She shrugged one shoulder, nodding once to let him know where she stood. He smiled, turning back to Gracie.

'I think that's a good idea, noodle,' he said, tugging on one of her locks. *Noodle*? 'How about you say goodbye to Maddie for now and hop in the car and I'll quickly ask Brooke when that can be?' Gracie wrapped her arms around his neck and nodded enthusiastically before bouncing back to Maddie. He stood.

'I have Saturday off,' she said—almost too easily. Hadn't she only just been talking about how she didn't want to fill her days off with playdates? But it seemed different with him, somehow.

Something flashed in his eyes—too quickly for her to identify what it was. 'Saturday sounds great,' he said. 'I'll shoot you a message later and we can decide what time and where, if you like.'

'Sure, I'll give you my number,' she started, grabbing for her phone.

'Already have it,' he teased.

She stood up straighter, her brow furrowed. *What*? How the hell could he have her number? She hadn't given it to him. This was the second time they'd talked, and she sure as hell knew she hadn't given it to him at the party or in the food court. 'How do y—'

He pulled his phone out of his pocket and seemed to flick through it. Then, he held the screen up to her. 'That's *your* number, isn't it?'

*Every single digit*. She nodded slowly, confused. 'Yes, but how …'

He rolled his phone around in his hands, his brow creased. 'The card you gave me for my birthday—it had that number under your name.'

*The card*. As in the card *her mother* had given her in the sealed envelope to give to him? The card she hadn't even bothered to look at what was written inside, thinking it was actually from her mother? *Shoot*. What else had her mother written in it?

'Oh, right, of course,' she mumbled. 'Well, I guess you … have … my number, after all.'

He considered her for a moment, then typed something into his phone. She heard her phone *ping* and he smiled. 'And now, you have mine.'

She smiled and started loading the kids in the car. Even as they said their goodbyes, and as he and Gracie waved to them as they pulled out of the carpark, and as she looked at his message—a smiley face with sunglasses—all she could think about was that damn card and whatever else was in it.

'Oh, damn it, Mother,' she whispered, the music in the car loud enough to drown out her voice. 'You played it well.'

And she had. Brooke couldn't question her mother about what was in the card, because then she'd know she'd talked to Lewis since the party. Well played, indeed.

Chapter 6

'I'm not going to lie, but that party was a kick in the balls.'

Lewis looked up from his sandwich to his friends. It seemed that Drew and Miles had been talking to him all morning, but he'd heard nothing. His mind was elsewhere. He swallowed the mouthful he had.

'I thought you two got some numbers,' he said, taking another bite.

Miles scoffed. 'No *real* ones.'

'They were all wrong numbers, apparently,' Drew said, rolling his eyes. 'That, or they had second thoughts and just pretended like they didn't know us.'

'Or they're such snobs they *actually* don't remember us.'

Lewis's eyebrow lifted. 'Sounds like those high-class girls can be mean,' he said.

'Gladys doesn't really want you with any of them, does she?' Drew said.

'Every single one of them would drive your mother insane,' Miles added, finishing off the pie he'd brought for lunch.

Lewis smiled, shrugging. 'They weren't *all* that bad,' he mumbled.

Drew and Miles shared a look before focussing back on him. 'I'm sorry, but were we looking at the same group of women?' Drew said. 'Because I'm pretty sure they were all that bad.'

Lewis leaned back against the wall, pulling his hat down over his face, closing his eyes for a moment. Fridays were usually easier going at work. Generally, the days seemed to pass pretty quickly, Fridays even more so. But since the party, after meeting Brooke, the days seemed to drag. And after bumping into her on Wednesday, the last two days had passed even slower than the rest of the week.

What were the odds of him bumping into her at the shops? That they just so happened to have a day off and be at the same place at the same time? Sure, he didn't usually have weekdays off—only if they finished a project early, which, to be honest, wasn't very often. He wondered if they'd crossed paths before but never noticed each other. It was possible they'd been at the same places at the same time, but he was sure he would have remembered her if he'd seen her. Surely, he would have felt the same as when he saw her at the presents table.

His mind drifted to the card she'd left, and her reaction when he reminded her that he had her number. She must have remembered she'd written her number at the bottom of the card, wouldn't she? So, why did she act like she didn't know? Or wondered how he had her number? Or perhaps she was wondering why he had her number in his phone but hadn't called or messaged her. Maybe she thought he had just been holding onto it for a rainy night. That would really make him look like an ass, wouldn't it?

Truth is, he'd put the number in his phone in case he built up the courage to ring her, or even send her a message. He didn't know why, since he'd been so adamant on not wanting to have a relationship. But it almost seemed better than not being able to get her out of his head without being able to see her again. Perhaps it was because he'd had questions of his own, like why she'd put her number in his card if she hadn't been looking for anything. And he'd stopped himself from calling a couple of times and deleted the messages before he could send it more than that. He hadn't known what to say, or what he wanted, or what he hoped would come out of him contacting her. But he didn't want to lose her number if he lost the card, and he wanted to have it on hand if he got the courage while he was out and about.

Maybe he just liked the idea of having the option there.

But, unless she was a good actor, she looked

genuinely surprised he had her number. Or maybe, like the other women at the party, she wasn't that much different and *forgot* she'd given out her number. He was still yet to decide on whether or not it was a good thing he'd bumped into her at the shops. Sure, bumping into anyone at the shops is coincidental. But then, he didn't *have* to suggest they had lunch together, and he wasn't entirely sure what convinced him to say it.

He assumed Gracie hugging Brooke when she saw her might have had something to do with it. But he'd been so determined to not have Gracie getting attached to anyone, yet having lunch with Brooke and her kids ... well, he figured that hadn't done him any favours. It was all Gracie could talk about on their way home—how great Brooke was, Maddie this, Maddie that, and how *cute* Ollie is. There was nothing Gracie had said that he could deny. And now she had the promise of a playdate to *keep* her talking about Brooke and her kids.

He wondered what led to them talking about Alice and Brett—it seemed a bit intense for a first actual conversation. Then again, the way they met hadn't been normal by any definition. He remembered how mad he felt when she told him about Brett, how he'd been such an asshole to her. He remembered wishing she didn't have to go through that, how he wanted to punch him for treating her so badly. He didn't know why he felt protective of her. He knew that kind of thing happened all the time. He guessed he just figured someone like Brooke deserved better.

Then again, if Brett had been a better guy, then perhaps he would never have met Brooke. Or he'd be pining over an unavailable woman.

He frowned. How had his mind got to that point? He wasn't looking for anything with anyone. He was focussed solely on Gracie, making sure she was happy and cared for and had a roof over her head, a bed to sleep in, and food in her stomach. He didn't have time for relationships, regardless of who it was with. And he had to remember that. He could not afford to forget that.

'Lewis?'

He lifted his hat up to face his friends, an annoyed look on their faces. He grimaced, knowing they must have been talking to him and he'd been completely out of it—focussing solely on Brooke. Again. *Shoot.*

'Hmm?'

'Who is she?' Drew said.

'Who?'

'The girl from the party who wasn't that bad,' Miles said in a tone that screamed repeating himself.

'Oh, just ... someone.'

Drew's eyebrow lifted. 'What did she look like?'

Lewis shrugged. 'Pretty, blonde hair.' Eyes that reminded him of rich honey and strong whisky. Hair that leaned more on the side of golden, rather than blonde. A body that had him imagining her every time he closed his eyes.

'Well, that narrows it down,' Miles said.

'You just described most of the people at the party,' Drew said.

'What was she wearing?' Miles added.

'Blue dress.' Spaghetti straps, flowers that were a slightly different shade of blue.

'Brings it down to about twenty people,' Miles said.

'Anything else?' Drew said.

'Runners.'

Drew and Miles looked at each other. 'Was anyone wearing runners?' Miles said.

'Wasn't one of the caterers, was it?' Drew said.

'They were all in black, idiot,' Miles said. 'Are you sure she was wearing runners?'

Lewis nodded slowly. 'What, weren't you looking at their shoes?' he teased.

'You do?' Drew said.

'In this case, yes.'

They sat in silence for a moment, Lewis polishing off his sandwich he'd still been holding onto. Once again, he found his mind drifting to whether or not he should message her. They *had*, after all, pencilled in a playdate for tomorrow when they saw each other at the shops. He had yet to actually message her about it. Again, every time he opened up his messages and went to type, he didn't know what to say.

He'd half-expected—hoped—she might have messaged first. At least that would give him a lead on what to say. But she hadn't. When he looked at their message conversation, all it showed was the smiley face wearing sunglasses. He wondered why he'd even sent that—out of anything he could have sent. He figured he just wanted to make sure it was actually her number and, well, anything would do in that message.

But since they had planned for a playdate for tomorrow and nothing had been organised yet, he figured he was probably going to have to come up with something to say. He just had to work out what, exactly that was.

'Hang on,' Miles said, snapping Lewis back to their conversation. 'She's not the one who was carrying Gracie about halfway through, is she?'

He nodded. 'Bingo.'

'Oh, *her*,' Drew added. 'But she looked bored at the party.'

'Exactly.'

'What did you say her name was?' Miles said, squinting.

'I didn't.'

'So, you'll tell us what she looked like, but not her name?' Drew said.

'I don't want it getting back to my mother,' he said simply. 'She'll look too far into it and start meddling again.'

'Would we tell her?' Drew said defensively.

He blinked at his friends and lifted his eyebrow. 'I'd hope not.'

'Wouldn't she find out anyway?' Drew said.

'No,' he said. 'Since it's not going to go anywhere.'

'Why not?' Miles said.

'Because she's not looking for anything and neither am I.'

'Sounds like you're perfectly suited for each other,' Drew scoffed.

'You know what you need?' Miles said.

Lewis rose to his feet, readying himself to get back to work now their lunch break was almost over. Miles and Drew followed suit. 'What?'

'You need to get laid.'

'That's the best idea I've heard all day,' Drew said.

Lewis shook his head. 'I don't have time for that.'

'You might find you'll have *more* time if you did,' Miles said.

Lewis laughed. 'How do you figure that?'

'Miles will say anything to justify sex,' Drew said. 'But seriously, there really is no harm in getting laid once in a while.'

'Maybe for you guys,' Lewis said. 'But I've got more at stake—and clearly, better morals.'

'You know you want to,' Miles said.

'And I'm interested in how you expect me to do it, anyway,' he added, frowning. 'Do you expect me to ask my *mother* to mind Gracie, just so I can get laid?'

Miles shrugged. Drew rubbed the stubble on his chin. 'Knowing Gladys, she might be on board with it.'

'No, she would tell me she taught me better than that.'

Drew waved his hand at him. 'Maybe years ago, but I bet she'd be on board with it now.'

'Then, you don't know Gladys well at all.'

'That girl,' Miles said, putting his hat on. 'She's not looking for anything, right? She'd be a perfect candidate for getting laid.'

Lewis shook his head, walking ahead of them. 'Kids are at stake, Miles,' he said.

'Haven't you heard of contraception?' Drew called out.

Lewis laughed, busying himself with work. He'd never been the kind of guy to just *get laid*. And even if he was, Brooke was definitely *not* the perfect candidate. The perfect candidate was someone you never wanted to see again and had a very slim chance of ever seeing again. A perfect candidate was someone who didn't have kids, who hadn't *met* Gracie. Brooke was a nice woman. Caring, sweet, funny, and someone who, despite his previous efforts, he still wanted to see again. *If* he ever slept with Brooke, it wouldn't be for the purpose of getting laid. It'd be so much more.

But he couldn't let it get that far. Ever.

They could be friends—they should be, for the sake of the kids. They might even become good friends, he might look forward to seeing her and try to see her more often. He might keep having dreams about her or wishing they could trial something more. But he could never act on that. There was *way* too much at stake. And Alice—what would that do to her memory? He'd made a promise to his wife. And he'd be damned if he didn't keep it.

***

Brooke stared at the blinking line on her phone. She couldn't say how long she'd been staring at it, but her guess would be that it was too long. How had she got to this point? Why should she feel annoyed he hadn't messaged her yet or felt like he didn't care at all? After all, it wasn't like the old days, where waiting for three days before calling was the norm. Besides, in any case, this was different. They had already agreed on a playdate tomorrow, and she was unsure if they were still going to go through with that. Not that it should matter. It would probably be better for everyone if they never saw each other again.

So why did she feel like she wanted to message him? Like she wanted to confirm she would, actually, be seeing him when he'd said they would? Why was she so determined to know whether or not he wanted anything to do with her? If she messaged him first, at least then she would have an answer. If he wanted to see her, he'd reply. If he wanted to know her, he'd say more in a message than simple answers.

But what the hell was she supposed to say?

She hadn't done this before. Not really. She didn't know what the done thing was, or how to talk to a guy she barely knew, *especially* when kids are involved. She sighed as her screen flicked to black.

Why should it matter to her, anyway? It's not as though she was looking for anything. Now, ever. With anyone.

'No message?'

Brooke jumped when her sister's voice seemed a whole lot closer than it should be. Sure enough, Georgie was practically peering over her shoulder. She sighed, frowning. Her sister was a quiet walker and had a habit of sneaking up on people. She would have thought that growing up with her would have made her immune, but it never did.

'Don't you ever give anyone warning?'

'What fun would that be?' Georgie said, flashing her sweet perfect smile. Georgie had long, luscious brown hair Brooke had always been jealous of, and a smile that could catch the attention of any man. Not to mention a body that had yet to be marred by pregnancy.

Georgie worked with Brooke when she wasn't travelling—a luxury Brooke would never really have. It's as though having kids completely ruined any chance of ever travelling and, well, she'd never really had the chance before kids. By the time she'd saved up almost enough money to travel, she fell pregnant with Maddie. She would never take it back, mind you. Maddie was her girl, her little best friend, even if she was on the brink of insanity some days. She loved her kids more than anything in the world, and though she sometimes wished things were a little different, or that she could have at least experienced *one* holiday, she never regretted having her kids.

'So, who is it?' Georgie urged, bumping her shoulder against Brooke's.

Brooke sighed, rolling her phone over in her hands, running her thumb over the pattern of the case on the back. 'No one.'

Georgie scoffed. 'Come on, I'm not *that* naïve,' she said. 'Are you waiting for a message, or trying to send one?'

'Either will do,' she admitted.

'Well, tell me more.'

Brooke stood up straighter, looking at her sister. 'You have to promise you won't tell Mum,' she said.

Georgie leaned back a little, feigning shock. 'Would I tell her?'

'Yes,' Brooke said, lifting an eyebrow.

Georgie's nose crinkled as she squinted. 'Okay, you're right, I probably would,' she admitted. 'But is it *that* important she doesn't know?'

'It's *imperative* she doesn't know.'

'Imperative?' Georgie laughed. 'Who even says that in normal conversation?'

Brooke frowned. 'I do,' she said, pressing her finger to her chest.

'But no one says it,' Georgie said, her eyes dancing. 'It's one of those words you'll see in writing, but not in casual conversation.' Brooke pinched the bridge of her nose. Georgie waggled her finger between them. 'I bet not many people even know what it means.'

'Most people know what it means,' Brooke said, bored. Georgie had another habit of directing the conversation to a different topic to avoid answering questions. At least Brooke had managed to pick up on *that* habit early on.

'But *no one* knows how to use it.' A triumphant look crossed over Georgie's face. 'It's like wench. No one knows how to use wench in casual conversation.'

'That's because it's from a totally different era.'

'My point is no one knows how to use imperative in a sentence the way it should.'

'I literally just did. And you're avoiding the topic.'

Georgie frowned. 'Why would I be avoiding the topic? You were just about to tell me who you're waiting to get a message from.'

'No,' Brooke said. '*You* were just about to promise me you won't tell Mum.'

'I'm sure we moved past that,' Georgie huffed. Brooke folded her arms across her chest, pressing her lips together. '*Fine*,' Georgie added. 'I won't tell her. Unless the topic comes up.'

'Georgie,' Brooke warned.

'And *if* the topic happens to come up,' Georgie said. 'I'll try my best to avoid telling her. But I won't blatantly lie to her if she asks me. She can see through my lies.'

'Everyone can see through your lies, Georgie.'

Georgie groaned. 'Is that a good enough promise?' Brooke bit her lip, then nodded. 'Good,' Georgie continued. 'Why don't you want Mum knowing, anyway?'

'Because she set it up,' Brooke mumbled.

Georgie's expression was puzzled, then her eyes widened in realisation. 'Oh, Gladys's boy?'

Brooke's mouth dropped open. 'You knew, and you didn't tell me?'

'How could I? I didn't see you before you went to the party and, by then, it was too late.'

'You have my number,' Brooke pointed out.

'Well, maybe I wanted to see how it turned out.'

'It hasn't,' Brooke said, holding up her phone. 'Clearly. Anyway, the message I'm waiting for isn't about … *that*. That's not going to happen.'

'I don't get it.'

Brooke sighed. 'I bumped into him at the shops a couple days ago,' she explained. 'We agreed to have a playdate tomorrow—for the kids. He said he'd message.'

'And he hasn't.'

She scrunched her nose up. 'It's probably for the best.'

'Is he with one of the other girls from the party?' Brooke squinted. 'Mum told me,' Georgie added quickly.

'I wouldn't know,' Brooke said, shrugging. 'I mean, he didn't look overly interested in any of the others, but I did leave early.'

Not that it should matter to her, but she hadn't really thought about *that* part until now. What if he was a lot more interested in the other women after she left? What if he was too busy organising dates with all the other women there to even spare her a second thought. They were all prettier than her. And though she was sure none of them were mothers or into kids, it was only a matter of time. Anyone could get used to the idea if they were given time.

Well, good for him, she thought. If he wanted to pursue a relationship with anyone, it wasn't up to her to decide who it was. And she'd made it painstakingly clear she wasn't looking for anything. Even if the thought of him with someone else made her insides burn. Perhaps it was good she might never hear from him again. Maddie would soon forget about their time at the shops and stop asking to see Gracie. But she was sure she would never forget about them. Lewis and Gracie had already made too much of an impact on her to forget about them. But maybe, one day, she'd stop dreaming about him.

'First impressions are important,' Georgie said, oblivious of the thoughts going through Brooke's head. 'If he didn't seem interested in them at the start, your odds are looking good. *Especially* if he wanted to see you tomorrow.'

Brooke shrugged, dropping her gaze to stare at the glass cabinet she was leaning on, staring at the glittering jewellery that was ridiculously overpriced and extravagant. It had been a quiet day—it never got overly busy working at a jewellers which had its pros and cons. Pros being that it wasn't a very stressful workplace. Cons being that there was *way* too much time to think.

'It was the kids, mostly,' she said. 'I think we were cornered into agreeing to a playdate.'

'Ahh,' Georgie said. 'So, basically, you're waiting to find out if it's still happening.' Brooke nodded. 'Message him, then.'

'I don't know what to say,' Brooke said, feeling her cheeks heat up, her voice hitting a pitch higher than was usual for her.

'Just ask him if you're still on for tomorrow,' Georgie said, leaning on the cabinet next to her.

'And if he doesn't respond?'

'Then, you'll have your answer,' Georgie said, shrugging. 'You like him, don't you?'

Brooke made a noise somewhere between a laugh and a scoff. 'I do not. What makes you think that?'

'Oh, please, I'm not an idiot,' Georgie said. 'You're already pining over the guy and it's over a *playdate*.'

Brooke crinkled her nose. 'Even so,' she said. 'Nothing is going to happen. I have already made that clear.'

'And why would you do that?'

'Because I'm not looking for anything.'

'Do you want my opinion?' Georgie said.

'Do I have a choice?'

'You need to get laid.'

Apparently, she didn't have a choice. She'd suspected not, since she never really did when it came to Georgie voicing her opinion. 'I do *not* need to get laid,' Brooke said, her eyes wide. 'Getting laid got me in this position.'

'Horny?'

Brooke whacked her sister on the arm, her cheeks reddening. 'Single—with kids.'

'Getting laid didn't get you there. A relationship did.'

Brooke frowned, turning to her friend. She'd met Maia when she started working at the jeweller's and they'd made fast friends. Georgie and Maia were closer, though, considering Brooke never had the time to catch up with them after work. Not when having kids made it near on impossible to let her hair down and relax, do what she wants.

'How much of that did you hear?' she asked.

Maia shrugged. 'Most of it,' she said, flashing a toothy grin. 'But Georgie's right. Relationships suck, getting laid doesn't.'

Brooke shook her head, trying not to smile. 'I don't have time for either.'

Georgie scoffed. 'You don't need time to get laid,' she said. 'And it makes you feel so much better afterwards.'

Brooke's mouth dropped as she stared at her sister. 'Do Mum and Dad know what you get up to?'

Georgie shrugged. 'Probably.' She squinted. 'But maybe don't mention it, in case they don't.'

Brooke laughed. If her parents knew what Georgie got up to, they would probably flip. Once upon a time, they might have expected it from Brooke—even though she was the good kid—but never from Georgie. Georgie had always been an angel at home, but Brooke was sure she was a bit of a party animal. She hadn't thought of her actually sleeping with guys, though. How her sister never ceased to surprise her.

'Well, I can't just go get laid,' Brooke said. 'I've got the kids to worry about.' Not to mention the fact finding someone to get laid with terrified her.

'I'll watch them for you,' Georgie said.

'What, at Mum and Dad's house?'

'Of course not,' Georgie said, pressing her hand to her chest. 'I'll watch them at your place.'

Brooke lifted an eyebrow. 'While I'm supposedly getting laid?'

'Oh, you won't be there,' Maia piped in.

'You're not suggesting I go back to his place, are you?'

'That's exactly what we're suggesting,' Georgie said.

'What if he has ... other ... intentions?'

'That's the whole point,' Georgie said.

'I mean something other than ... getting laid.'

'Like if he's an axe murderer?' Maia offered.

Brooke stretched her arm out towards Maia, still facing Brooke. '*Especially* if he's an axe murderer.'

'Not helping, Maia,' Georgie scolded. 'Oh, come on, Brooke. I've gone home with plenty of guys and I'm still here. You'll be fine.'

'I'm not doing it,' Brooke said, decidedly.

'Because you've already got your man?' Maia said, nudging her shoulder.

'We're only going to be friends,' she said defensively.

'But she likes him,' Georgie said, winking at Maia.

Brooke sighed. 'I don't know, okay? But it won't work, anyway.'

'Because of the kids?' Georgie said.

Brooke shrugged. She didn't like blaming the kids for anything like this, but in a way, yes, it was. She didn't want to have the kids get attached to anyone and have it not work out. Maddie had already been through that with Brett—and she had been younger then. It was bound to affect her more now, especially if there was another kid involved. Like Gracie. No, she and Lewis could only be friends. It was the only way it could work with them. The only way to avoid breaking more hearts than two. The only way to avoid destroying a potentially good friendship she could have with him.

She flicked her phone back on and typed out a quick message asking him if they were still on for tomorrow and hit the send button. She turned the screen back off before she started freaking out about messaging him first and tucked it into her pocket, looking up at the speculating eyes of Georgie and Maia.

'What?' she said.

'Look at you go, you wench,' Georgie said, winking. 'See? I can totally use it in a sentence.'

Brooke shook her head, turning to walk to the back room to get back to work. 'Not what you're thinking,' she called over her shoulder. 'And not the right context, either!'

Even if the thought of simply seeing him made her nervous.

*Chapter 7*

'Shoot, shoot, shoot,' she mumbled, pulling into the first free carpark she could find. She was late. *Shoot.*

Brooke jumped out of the car almost as soon as the engine had stopped running. After all her worrying the last few days as to whether or not Lewis was going to message her, it seemed the thing she had to worry about was whether or not she'd actually make it in time. He'd been quick to respond to her message yesterday—almost too quick. It was as though he'd already had a message typed out and was just about to send it.

He'd suggested that new place in town that was filled with trampolines—perfect for kids, apparently, though she hadn't been. Apparently, they also had a section for the littlies and seats close by for spectators to enjoy a coffee. He'd suggested they go as soon as they were open to avoid the crowd. She thought that was a good idea—especially since being around crowds with the kids running loose was not exactly her idea of fun.

She unclipped Maddie from her seat and swung the stroller out of the boot—just in case she needed it—and pulled Ollie out of his seat, choosing to carry him inside instead of struggling with that damned five-point harness that seemed to be the standard now. She chucked her bag and Ollie's backpack on the stroller and navigated her way towards the door, relieved when someone held it open for her. Not just someone—Lewis.

She was out of breath, flushed, exhausted, tired, frazzled, and was certain she'd already started sweating. It wasn't even time for morning tea yet! She was worried he wouldn't have waited since she was almost twenty minutes late, but here he was, holding the door open for her, a smile on his face, looking especially *fine*. She was willing to bet he, at least, would have got more than a few hours of sleep last night. She was carrying Ollie around his waist, which was a position he seemed to think he was a superhero in, and she was well aware she probably looked a mess, but she smiled at him.

'Morning,' he said as she reached him. 'I saw you getting out of the car and thought you might need a hand.'

She groaned, then felt her cheeks flush from embarrassment. 'Sorry I'm late,' she said, nudging a babbling Ollie up a little as though indicating to him. 'This guy threw some curveballs right when I was about to leave.'

Like staying asleep even after Maddie had woken up—she supposed because he didn't sleep half the night—and having a full nappy explosion requiring a quick bath and an entire outfit change when she should have been walking out the door.

He shrugged, smiling. 'But you made it,' he said, handing a pair of socks to Maddie. 'Good morning, Maddie,' he added. 'Gracie's already inside. Do you want to pop those on and join her?'

Maddie made an excited noise, taking the socks from his hand and racing ahead. Brooke pushed the stroller through the door and he followed her inside. She could practically feel his closeness behind her and felt a strange sense of loss when he moved to her side with some distance between them.

'They're special socks or something,' he said. 'Honestly, I don't see how they really differ from normal ones, but they just *have* to have them. I ... hope ... you don't mind, but I paid for Maddie while I was paying for Gracie. Some card limit on their machine or something. Ollie gets in free. I didn't get any coffee yet—I wasn't sure how long you'd be.'

He visibly took a deep breath and smiled again. She tried to smile back but found her lips were already curved up as high as they would go. Was *he* blathering? And here she was thinking she was the one that talked too much when she was nervous. Or maybe her being so late gave him a bit too much time to think.

'I believe it's my turn to pay, anyway,' she teased, feeling her cheeks flush again at the flirtatious undertone.

His smile dropped. 'I don't mind shouting, really,' he said quickly.

'It's my turn, Lewis,' she said, wondering when she'd got to the point of arguing about who was paying for who.

She'd never really worried about anyone shouting her and the kids before—being a single working mother, she generally had to save every penny she could get. Then again, someone offering to shout her and the kids was very rare these days, especially since she never really went out *that* much. She cleared her throat, feeling her heart skip a beat.

'Besides,' she added. 'You can pay next time.'

He considered her for a moment, then his smile returned, slightly higher on one side that made her breath catch and her body heat up a degree. Was it hot inside? Or was that just her? He lifted his hands, facing his palms towards her.

'If you insist,' he said, his eyes flashing. He nodded towards Ollie. 'Want me to take him while you get the coffee, then?'

She hesitated a second, not because she didn't trust him—though, did she?—but because she knew Ollie was very much a mama's boy. He'd only just stopped being *as* dependent on her, but throw another person in the mix and he's back to square one. She was certain she'd be embarrassed if Ollie screamed the whole time Lewis had him, but she was willing to risk it to have even a minute of not having to lug his little body around. He didn't weigh *that* much—no more than ten kilos—but he could certainly start to feel heavy pretty quickly, especially when he started squirming like he was doing now. Decidedly, she turned that side towards Lewis, lifting Ollie to make it easier.

'He'll probably start screaming, but if *you* insist,' she said, passing him over.

Lewis tucked his arm under Ollie, holding him to his side, Ollie's arm resting on his shoulder. She felt a strange feeling she couldn't quite place. Perhaps a slight amount of uncertainty, that weird feeling when someone else is holding the child you're used to having attached to your hip.

'Ahh,' Lewis hummed, furrowing his brow as he turned his head to face Ollie. 'You're a mama's boy, are you?'

Ollie frowned at him, examining his face as though he wasn't yet sure of how he felt. His gaze dropped to Lewis's jaw—covered in a neatly trimmed few-day growth—and his eyes widened. He hadn't started screaming yet, which was a plus. But he hadn't been around much facial hair, considering Brooke's dad was always clean-shaven. Instinctively, it seemed, Lewis lifted his hand and stroked his chin, frowning back at Ollie.

'Nah, you're all right,' Lewis said in a tone that seemed to vibrate through Brooke, even though he was talking to her son. 'We're mates, aren't we?' He turned to face her, indicating to the stroller. 'Want me to take that?'

She stared at him for a moment, briefly unsure of what was going on. Why hadn't Ollie started screaming yet? *Especially* with Lewis holding him! He wasn't used to being held by a man, for starters, except for Brooke's dad, and especially not one with facial hair. Perhaps it was the facial hair delaying the screams since he was fixated with it. She watched as Ollie lifted a hand slowly and moved it towards Lewis's chin, retracting his hand before it could connect. Unsure of why it made her feel jealous, she nodded slowly, nudging the stroller towards him, and grabbing her bag from it so she could pay for the coffee.

Lewis smiled, turning the stroller with one hand with an ease that was impossible for Brooke when she used *both* hands. As he walked towards the table near what looked to be the little kids' section, Ollie looked over Lewis's shoulder. She was convinced she saw his lip quiver before he started crying. Somehow, him crying made her feel better. She couldn't have Ollie getting too attached as well.

'Mama!' Ollie screamed, reaching his little hand out towards her.

'Mama?' Lewis repeated, pulling a face at Ollie. Ollie focussed back on him, glancing uncertainly back at Brooke every few seconds. 'Mama's over there,' Lewis added, pointing towards her. 'Do you like jumping?' Ollie stopped crying, sticking his forefinger and thumb in his mouth. Lewis bounced Ollie on his hip. 'Jumping? Yeah?' Ollie made his affirmative grunt and nodded his slow, deep nods, bringing a smile to Brooke's face. 'All right, jumping it is.'

Brooke kept watching for a second as Lewis parked the stroller at the table and carried Ollie over to the little kids' section and stood Ollie on the little trampoline, holding his hands as Ollie carefully started bouncing. She felt a warmth spread through her chest she knew shouldn't be there. Lewis had a kid of his own—of course, he would be good at distracting them. Still, she couldn't help it. He wasn't just entertaining *any* kid. He was entertaining *her* kid. She heard a throat clear and turned around to see the cashier waiting impatiently at the register. It took her a few awkward seconds to remember what she was supposed to be doing.

God, how could she really be friends with Lewis if she was already feeling like this? It was dangerous, unchartered territory, and it terrified her.

***

He hadn't been waiting for long, truth be told, but he didn't admit that to Brooke. They'd been on time, to start with, then he realised he'd forgotten his wallet, so he had to go back home to pick it up. By then, he was running late. But since Brooke messaged him saying she was running late, his goal became getting there before she did. And he had. About five minutes, to be exact. He'd briefly worried Brooke had been and gone in that time, but figured, even if she had, he and Gracie may as well stay anyway. He made a point of doing something with Gracie on his days off. It's just that, this time, Brooke and her kids were also going to be there.

He'd be lying if he said she didn't look frazzled when she got there. But even so, she still looked beautiful, and seeing her made his heart quicken in ways it shouldn't. Especially since he'd decided they could only be friends. And the way she suggested there'd be a next time, using his words to make sure of it, it made him happier than it should.

Offering to take Ollie made sense to him. She'd need her hands free for the coffee and, considering Ollie had already been wriggling to free himself from her grip, he figured he may as well make it easier on her. He'd half expected Ollie would have started screaming the second he realised he was in Lewis's arms instead of his mother's. He hadn't really held anyone else's kids before, only Gracie. So, he wouldn't really know how they were supposed to react. But he figured most kids didn't like other people holding them.

But Ollie had surprised him by focussing on him—his jaw, mostly. He suspected he hadn't been around much facial hair before, judging by the look he was getting. He figured kids can either go two ways when it came to facial hair—extreme terror, or intense fascination. As it turned out, Ollie leaned more on the latter. Thank God. He wasn't sure he could deal with a howling child that was terrified of him.

He managed to get Ollie interested in the little

play area enough to sneak back to the table at the same time as Brooke. He glanced towards the bigger trampolines, watching Maddie and Gracie jumping around together. So far, they had the whole place to themselves, but he knew it was only time before more people arrived. It had partially been Gracie's idea to go trampolining. He'd still been trying to decide on the best place to have a playdate when he remembered Gracie mentioning the time they'd gone when they opened and said she wanted to go again.

He'd finally settled on a message and was about to send it when he'd got a message from Brooke asking if they were still on for their playdate. He'd had to adjust his message slightly, but it was otherwise the same. Then he'd wondered if he should have delayed sending the message a few minutes, so it didn't come across as desperate. But it was too late now. It had well and truly been done, and here they were, at their playdate, and he was feeling like he was enjoying it a whole lot more than he should be.

He slid into the seat next to Brooke—perfect for both of them to see each of the kids. And he wouldn't complain about sitting next to her, even if it was borderline not-just-friends. She casually shifted in her seat, putting an inch or so more distance between them, and he couldn't shake the disappointed feeling. Even if he shouldn't feel it at all.

'So,' she said. It looked as though she was

attempting to be casual, but he noticed the slight shake in her voice. 'Been busy?'

He nodded slowly. 'Since Wednesday?' he teased. 'Work, mostly. You?'

'Work,' she said, staring at Ollie playing by himself.

He reached for his coffee, taking a sip, scalding his mouth, and feeling the burn down his throat. Usually, he was okay with hot drinks. But he mostly had them sitting for a few minutes before he drank. He cleared his throat.

'Sorry about the late notice,' he said. 'I lost track of time, blinked, and it was Friday.'

'Oh, no, I get it,' she said, waving her hand towards him. 'It was the same for me.'

He lifted his eyebrow, taking a slower sip of his coffee. Prepared, this time, for it being hot. It may have been a bit of a lie. Truth is, the last few days had taken longer than any other day he could remember. But he also felt like he had to justify not messaging her until so late and, well, that was the best excuse he could come up with. He wondered if she was the same, or if it actually did pass quickly for her. He tried to ignore the little bit of hope that it was the former.

He dropped his gaze to her hands, twisted together in her lap. Her knuckles were white as she twisted them tighter and, when he focussed back on her face, her eyelids were heavy, her face pale.

'Are you okay?' he asked.

She turned to face him, her eyes widening, and

he felt his breath catch at the striking colour of her eyes. God, how could he be friends with her? 'Of course,' she said. 'Why wouldn't I be?'

'You just look … tired,' he said, squinting. 'Beautiful, of course, but … tired.'

Her eyes widened a little more and she dropped her gaze, her cheeks reddening, his words catching up to him. *Beautiful*? Well, of course, she was. There was no denying it. She was quite possibly the most beautiful specimen he'd ever seen. But he still shouldn't have said it. Especially if he was wanting to stay just friends with her. He glanced over towards the girls and watched them jumping between trampolines. His mind drifted back to Alice. He'd once thought she was the most beautiful woman he'd ever meet. And he'd once been convinced he'd never even dream of being close to someone else.

'I … umm,' Brooke said, clearing her throat. 'Ollie's still not sleeping through. I didn't get much sleep last night.'

He stared at his cup. He'd been lucky enough to have Gracie sleeping through from early on. Simply caring for a baby was exhausting enough, he couldn't imagine having another kid now who didn't sleep through. Gracie had been hard enough—and she was an easy baby, so he'd been told, anyway.

'And being his age, he's teething and going through some kind of sleep regression or something,' she continued. 'I don't know. I've never really been able to keep up with it.'

'I know what you mean,' he said.

She sighed, taking a sip of her coffee. 'I just know he's never been a good sleeper, and now he's worse.'

'I still can't keep up with Gracie,' he said. 'It's always something, isn't it? The attitude ...'

'Oh, God, the *attitude*!' she said, smiling at him, her eyes dancing. He smiled back, wondering if that meant their awkward start was over with. 'I swear I have a teenage girl in my house already.'

'At least you're better equipped to deal with a teenage girl than I am,' he said.

Her mouth dropped open, her eyes wide. 'Oh, I'd say you're a lot safer than I am.'

'You're a woman though, you know how to deal with the ... stuff.'

Her eyebrow lifted, her lips curved into a smile. 'I forgot you're an only child.'

His brow furrowed. 'What's that got to do with anything?'

'I mean, you don't have a sister,' she said. 'So, I'll pass it off as blissful ignorance.'

'I don't understand,' he said, shaking his head. What was she getting at?

She dropped her head back a little, her smile broad. 'You haven't experienced the ticking time bomb of a teenage girl. Not to mention the whole mother-daughter relationship that accompanies it.'

He raised an eyebrow. 'Surely, not every teenage girl is a ticking time bomb.'

She nodded her head. '*Every* teenage girl,' she said. 'I remember my dad spending a *lot* of time out of the house when my sister and I were teenagers.'

'You? No,' he said, drawing out the syllables. She laughed, a rich sound that made his stomach clench. 'What did he do when he was out of the house?'

'Picked up some extra shifts where he could,' she said. 'He worked for a manufacturing company, so there was usually work available. Other than that, he took on a few hobbies and got fit from cutting laps around the block.'

'It couldn't have been *that* bad,' he said, hoping that it at least wouldn't be with Gracie.

'Oh, it was *that* bad,' she said. 'We used to argue a lot. Something with all the hormones flying around the house, I suppose.'

'That doesn't sound like fun,' he admitted.

She shrugged. 'It's how it goes,' she said. 'I don't know, you might get away with it to a point, considering it's just you and Gracie, but don't hold your breath. There will likely be difficult times.'

He laughed. 'I hope it's not that bad,' he said. 'Do you have a plan on how you'll deal with it?'

'Oh, I thought I did,' she said. 'Had all my comebacks worked out, but I've already used them all on my five-year-old, so I think I'll be in trouble when she actually is a teenager.'

He smiled, even if, inside, he was freaking out a little about Gracie becoming a teenager. It was still years away, but somehow, it didn't seem that far off. He'd already been getting that little girl attitude, he couldn't imagine what it would be like when she's a teenager. Hopefully, it wouldn't be as bad as Brooke was making it out to be.

'What kind of things did you argue about?' he said. 'Just so I'm prepared.'

'Anything and everything,' she said, shaking her head. 'There really is no preparing for it. But they do eventually grow out of it.'

'Yeah?'

She nodded. 'Roughly when they move out and have kids of their own,' she teased. 'At least then there's proper substance to the arguments and they're not as intense.'

'Like?'

She pursed her lips as if thinking, and he thought it was cute. He wondered what her lips would feel like against his and felt the guilt as he diverted his gaze. How could he think about kissing another woman when he'd married Alice? He had to remember he'd made a promise, a decision, that he wouldn't love another woman. He couldn't do that to Alice, to Gracie. Even if his mother pushed it.

'Like,' she said, drawing it out thoughtfully. 'Like getting laid, for example.' He felt his eyebrow shoot up. 'Well, not in the ones with Mum,' she added, talking quickly. 'But Georgie, she seems so convinced it would solve all my problems.' She laughed awkwardly. 'She's *so* adamant I should ... I—' She froze, a look of horror crossing her face. He guessed she'd only *just* realised what she'd been talking about. 'Oh, God,' she said slowly, covering her face with her hands.

He smirked.

How could he not?

***

Mortified.

To put it simply.

She was mortified.

How could she have been blabbing on about how her sister thought she had to get laid to the guy she hadn't been able to stop thinking about? She'd brushed aside that conversation with Georgie and Maia, doing her best to forget about it. And if she hadn't forgotten about it, it was to remain only in her head. Top secret. Never to utter a single word about it. And here she was, telling him *everything* about it.

She was sure her face was redder than it had ever been before, and she could tell he was amused with her rambling. Even if she'd briefly thought of him as a possibility if she'd ever been into just getting laid. But it would be way too complicated with him.

He cleared his throat, sounding as though he was stifling a laugh. 'So, in summary, your sister thinks you should get laid?'

She groaned, feeling her cheeks growing hotter. *Of course,* he wasn't going to let that go. He was a guy. And from what she knew of guys, topics of anything sex-related are amusing. But she'd rather not at her expense.

'You know, it's funny you say that,' he added. She risked a glance up at him and felt her breath catch in her throat at the intensity in his eyes. 'My mates were saying that's what I needed, too. I figured they didn't understand how the very concept of kids makes that impossible.'

She nodded, not sure she could actually find any words to say without making more of a fool of herself. He still held her gaze with his gorgeous eyes, and she could have sworn he was, somehow, a little closer. She could feel her heart practically pounding out of her chest and hoped he couldn't hear it. *This was dangerous territory*. She had to remember that.

'Not that I'm that kind of guy, anyway,' he added, clearing his throat again. 'I'm not. Never have been. You?' She looked at him questioningly, her brow furrowed. 'Into that, I mean. Has it ever been your scene?' She shook her head. 'So, then, it's pointless anyway, right? They don't know what they're talking about.'

He diverted his gaze towards the bigger trampolines and she shifted her gaze to Ollie. He was pressed up against the glass fence watching the girls bouncing on the trampolines. She'd bet he wanted to join them rather than stay in the little kids' section. Heck, *she* was feeling like she wanted to join the girls. Anything to stop making a fool of herself.

'Right,' she muttered, looking back at Lewis. 'Do you think the word imperative can be used in casual conversation?'

He frowned, focussing back on her. 'What?'

'Imperative,' she repeated. 'Can it be used in casual conversation?'

He shrugged. 'Why wouldn't it?'

She smiled. 'Just wondering.'

Chapter 8

'Daddy?'

'Yes, noodle?'

'I had fun at the trampoline place with Maddie and Brooke and Ollie.'

Lewis stroked Gracie's hair back from her face, making sure her blankets were tucked tightly around her, and she had her favourite snuggle bear she'd slept with every night since she was born. Alice had picked it out—pink because they knew they were having a girl—and it was one of the few things of Alice's he'd been able to keep. The rest had either been too heartbreaking to keep or had broken over the years. Her parents had taken most things off his hands. But the fact that toy had become Gracie's absolute favourite meant she always had a part of her mother with her. Even if she never really understood until she was older.

'So did I, sweetheart,' he said, bending down to press a kiss to her forehead.

Lewis and Brooke hadn't had much of a chance to go into too much conversation, especially after the one about how people thought they should both get laid. He had to admit, it was pretty funny they'd both coincidentally had similar conversations with different people, but still, clearly off the cards for both of them. After that, the trampoline place had a rush of people come in, making it way too crowded to be comfortable and Ollie started acting up again. Even though it seemed to go a whole lot quicker than he'd thought, he still couldn't help but feel a little disappointed when they left. Apparently, so had Gracie.

She'd been on a hype from their playdate all day, raving on and on about how much fun Maddie is, how Maddie is her new best friend, and please, please, *please*, can they do it again. It might have driven him crazy if he hadn't already been thinking about it himself.

There was a moment there when he'd wondered what it would be like to kiss her. When he'd thought about being more than friends with Brooke. And it terrified him. She was an incredible woman—he could see that. He didn't need to know everything about her to see she was different from most other women. She was genuine, honest, and blathered when she was nervous. She liked coffee and kebabs the same way he did—what more was there? A lot, he imagined. A whole lot more of Brooke to unveil and discover. And he wanted to do just that. He couldn't help it.

He couldn't help that he wanted to sit next to her in hopes her leg might bump against his, or her shoulder might brush past his. He couldn't help that all he could think about was having her close enough to maybe sneak a kiss. He couldn't shake the feeling of wanting to wake up next to her, even when he hardly knew her. And he couldn't quite place it, whether it was the loneliness of not having someone to spend his nights with, or the need to have someone he could talk to and be close to. But there was something about Brooke he was finding irresistible, and at the same time, made his gut clench.

How could he feel this way about anyone? How could he even *think* about it? He couldn't dishonour Alice's memory like that. Already, he was struggling to remember what Alice looked like without the help of a photograph. And it's all because of Brooke. But they were already too involved to cut it away. Gracie and Maddie were friends—at the very least, he and Brooke had to be friends, too. But God, it would be hard for him.

'Can we have another playdate?' Gracie asked, snuggling down in her bed.

Lewis bit into his lip. 'Would you like that, noodle?'

Gracie nodded. 'Maddie's my *best* friend. I wish I

could see her *all* the time.'

He smiled, laughing softly. 'I'm sure we could arrange another playdate.'

Gracie smiled her toothy childish grin, then her face grew serious. She tucked her bear up under her chin, holding it closer. 'Is … is Brooke going to be my new mummy?'

He frowned, even though his heart skipped a beat. 'Why do you say that?'

Gracie shrugged, her lip quivering. 'Because I don't have a mummy. Isn't that why Nanna threw that party for you? To find me a new mummy?'

He felt something stick in his throat and his eyes started burning. He sat on the edge of the bed, stroking her hair again. 'Sweetheart, you have a mummy, remember? We've talked about this before.'

'But my real mummy isn't here.'

In the dim light of the nightlight, he could see her eyes glistening. It tore at him. He pressed his hand to her chest. 'She's in here,' he said. 'She always will be.'

'But it's not the same,' Gracie said quietly.

He swallowed the lump in his throat. He knew it wasn't the same as having her here. God, he knew it all too well. But he also didn't want to replace Alice, and if being with someone meant, in Gracie's mind, Alice was being replaced, then he wasn't sure he could go through with it.

'I know, noodle,' he said. 'But it's all we have.'

Gracie's lip quivered. 'I like Brooke,' she said.

'Maddie said she's a good mummy, and she's really nice to me.'

Lewis felt his jaw clench. What could he say? He was torn inside. How could he explain to a five-year-old it wasn't going to happen? So much for not having her grow attached to Brooke. *Shoot.*

'I'm sure she is,' he said. 'But she's not your mummy.'

'But she could be,' Gracie said defiantly. 'I'd like her to be.'

He rose to his feet, adjusting her blankets again. 'Try to get some sleep, Gracie,' he said, planting another kiss on her forehead. Gracie pouted but didn't respond until he was near the door.

'Maddie doesn't have a daddy, either,' she sulked. 'I bet she'd like you to be her daddy.'

He rubbed his forehead, pausing at the door. What had gotten into Gracie? This whole thing had never been an issue before. Why now? The party, of course. It had to be. His meddling mother putting ideas in Gracie's head. Well, it wasn't going to work. Even if it tore at his chest and made his heart ache. He'd promised himself—promised Alice—there was no one else for him. And for five years, he'd held true to that. Why should it be any different now?

'Maddie has a daddy,' he said, his voice low. 'And you have a mummy.'

'But—'

'Goodnight, Gracie,' he said. 'No more talking about it tonight.'

'Goodnight, Daddy,' she said, sulkily.

He left her room, trying to ignore the urge to go back in, gather her up in his arms and promise her he'd do absolutely anything to make her happy. Truth is, he wasn't sure he was ready to do *that*. He'd always given her whatever she wanted, within reason. But this was something he just couldn't give her. Not like that. He didn't want to replace Alice in Gracie's life. He'd worked so hard to make sure her memory could be kept alive. And now, he was wondering if even that had been a good idea.

He grabbed a beer from the fridge and went to the lounge room, settling in on the couch and rubbing his eyes. He sighed, dropping his hand, staring at the room around him. When had his house started to seem empty? Obviously, he'd first noticed it the first night Alice didn't come home. But after he'd brought Gracie home, it hadn't seemed so empty. There'd always been that something missing, but it had never bothered him.

Now, the emptiness was back.

Was Gracie happy? Had he been wrong in assuming that keeping Alice's memory alive would be beneficial for Gracie? He never thought it was the easy path to take, but he also didn't want to lie to his daughter. And now, she was talking about finding a new mummy. Well, it's not that simple. And even if it was, it wasn't a matter of simply finding a new mother. He'd have to find someone who was willing to be a mother figure, without replacing Alice's memory. And he wasn't sure that was something any woman would really be willing to do.

So, why couldn't he get Brooke out of his head? He figured it was probably because she's the one Gracie had in mind. And he was sure she would be a good mother figure—he could see she was a good mother to her own kids. But he couldn't ask that of her. And even if he could, he wasn't sure he was ready.

Still, they didn't have to be *together* for her to be a good mother figure for Gracie. And maybe that part wouldn't be so bad. Even if the very thought of it ate at him in a way he wasn't sure what it meant. He took a long, slow sip of his beer and rolled his phone around in his hand.

Being friends with Brooke meant she'd be in Gracie's life. Naturally, she'd have a motherly influence on her. It wouldn't be taking anything away from Alice—not really. But he was becoming more and more unsure about whether or not *he* could be friends with Brooke, without it taking anything away from Alice. Already, she'd started affecting his memories of Alice. He'd once thought it might be inevitable—that one day, her memories would begin to be not so clear. But he'd also been determined to avoid that happening. And now, he had no choice, because it was happening.

And it could be purely coincidental he'd met Brooke at the same time as his memories of Alice began to fade. It had been five years, after all. But why did he still feel that ache of guilt? The feeling he was losing whatever he had left of Alice?

He had to put Gracie first. Even if it near on killed

him.

*** 

Brooke eased the bedroom door almost closed, leaving a gap wide enough to let in a trickle of light, and tip-toed to her lounge room where she had a glass of wine and a good book waiting for her. Truth is, she was so exhausted from getting the kids to bed she was sure she wouldn't be able to concentrate on her book, anyway.

Maddie was good at bedtimes, even though she was still on a hype from their playdate that morning. On the other hand, Ollie seemed to be at that awkward transition age where two naps in the day meant he put up a fight to go to sleep at night, and he just couldn't last the day on one nap. She remembered that stage with Maddie. She'd been convinced it was the beginning of the end of her and Brett, but looking back on it now, it might have all started before then. Brett hadn't been faithful, and as it turned out, he wasn't much of a family guy. Too bad it took having a family for him to realise that.

She slipped her reading glasses on and sat her laptop on her lap. She basically needed to defrag to even be in a mood to read. She opened up the internet browser and started searching on the supermarket's website, putting in her order to collect the next day—she'd practically given up physically going into the shop to get more than just a few things after having kids. And even on the days where she only needed a few things, she tried to do it without the kids. She imagined it wouldn't be so bad taking the kids if she had someone with her, but by herself, she avoided it as much as possible.

Her phone dinged, and she picked it up, surprised to see a message from the last person she expected it to be from—Lewis. She put her phone on silent, so she wouldn't wake the kids and opened it, sipping her wine.

*What you up to?*

She smiled, feeling goofy. She shouldn't, should she? It's not like she was in school anymore, getting messages from the guy she was crushing on. Still, there was something in seeing his name pop up on her screen that made her heart skip a beat.

She took another sip of wine and tapped out a reply. *Just got the kids to bed. Settling in for the night with some wine, a book, and some online shopping. You?*

She hit send and bit into her lip, staring at the screen. She certainly wouldn't be able to focus on her book now. Another message popped up on the screen.

*Same. Minus the wine and the online shopping. I don't suppose you know where my glasses are, do you?*

She felt her smile widen, though she couldn't work out why. *On top of the fridge?*

*Why would they be on the fridge?*

She laughed. *I put them there sometimes—out of reach of the kids, I guess.*

*That's a weird place to put them.*

She nibbled at her bottom lip, forgetting about the online shop for now. Her fingers hesitated over her screen before she tapped out another message. *I can't imagine you wearing glasses.*

She stared at the screen for a minute before she realised she was holding her breath. Another minute passed and there was still no reply, as opposed to his other messages that were quicker than this. She sipped her wine, forcing herself to put her phone down. It wasn't flirting, was it? She hadn't meant for it to seem like she was, but reading back on it, it could come across that way. Heck, some of *his* messages seemed like flirting. That, or she was out of practice.

She took a deep breath and tried to focus on her online shop but only ended up staring at her laptop screen. And when her phone buzzed next to her, she might have grabbed it too quickly.

*They were on top of the fridge.*

She laughed, then felt her breath catch when a picture popped up after the message. He was wearing black-rimmed, not-quite-square glasses, and *God*, they suited him. She felt something stir inside her, despite her efforts and squashing the feeling. He was a handsome guy—there was no denying it. And she'd be lying if she said she wasn't attracted to him. But she couldn't go there, could she?

She had the kids to think about—Maddie and Ollie—and he had Gracie. Besides, he'd indicated he wasn't looking for anything, and neither was she.

This was just a friendship. With a guy that made her heart skip a beat and gave her butterflies. Oh, God, how could she do this? Another message popped up on the screen and it didn't help her confusion one bit.

*I can't imagine YOU wearing glasses.*

Her breaths were coming quick and shallow. Choppy. It made sense, right? He'd sent her a picture, it was simply common courtesy to send one back. And it's not as though they were ... rude ... or unsuitable for prying eyes. Even though she planned on keeping that picture of him entirely to herself. He simply wanted to see what her glasses looked like. On her. Heck, he'd even worded it the same as she absent-mindedly had.

Before she could change her mind again, she flicked to her camera and took a selfie. Then another, since the first one was less than flattering. Then, she sent it and forcefully put her phone on the couch next to her, taking a deep breath. It was totally normal, it had to be. Friends send pictures to each other all the time. At least, she thought they did. And she'd keep convincing herself of it. Her phone buzzed again, and she hesitated a moment before checking her messages.

*You're beautiful.*

She took in a sharp breath and put her phone back down. Oh, boy, she was in trouble. How was she even supposed to reply to that? She stared at her online shop, trying to get it sorted so at least *something* was organised in her life. But all she could think about was his messages. Hadn't it started as a completely innocent conversation? Probably the same as how their others had been. But even those had managed to tread on topics that were not casual and not entirely innocent.

But it was rude for her not to reply, wasn't it? She picked up her phone and tapped out a quick *thank you* before putting it back down. She wouldn't look at it again until her online order was done, at least. She couldn't. And if she didn't look at it again all night, that would probably be for the better. She would simply forget she'd conversed with him at all and she would sleep well. She had to. She couldn't allow herself to become frazzled or read too much into this. Her phone buzzed again, and she tried her best to ignore it, but once again, her eyes drifted almost instinctively towards it instead of staying on her computer.

'Damn it,' she muttered, giving in to the temptation. She picked up her phone and flicked over to the message.

*Gracie wants another playdate.*

She smiled, wondering if he'd heard of nothing else but begging for another playdate as she'd had from Maddie. These kids just seemed to not understand the concept of waiting for a while before asking for another playdate. Maddie had started up in the car on the way home. She wondered when Gracie started on Lewis. Her phone buzzed again, and she smiled. Maybe he'd been feeling the same way she felt when he took longer to reply before.

*Are you free Saturday?*

Her fingers hesitated before tapping out a reply. *It's my day off.*

She figured he knew that too well. Why else would he suggest it for another playdate? She'd already told him what days she had off. Another message popped up on her screen.

*I know. Are you doing anything?*

*No.*

*I was thinking we could go to the pool, since the weather's warmer.*

Swimming? That could work. She knew Maddie loved the pool, and Ollie enjoyed a paddle, too. Chances are, they wouldn't even have much of a chance to talk. And she *had* been thinking about taking the kids to the pool when she found enough energy. Like going to the shop, it would be easier with another person there.

*Sounds good*, she replied.

A few more minutes passed before she got a response. She bit into her lip as she read it.

*I was also thinking we could meet up for dinner sometime this week.*

She reread the message, then read it again. What was wrong with their playdate on Saturday? Sure, if it was with the purpose of placating the kids until Saturday. It would have to be an early dinner, she thought. Otherwise, Ollie would get cranky. But if she thought about it, she couldn't really remember the last time she went *out* for dinner. Sure, she'd been to her parents' place, and she'd been to places for lunch. But dinner? Where would they even go?

*Do you know of anywhere kid-friendly?*

She waited for his reply, and when she got it, she realised she might not have been looking too far into it at all. Rather, she'd completely missed what he was asking. And she had no idea what it would mean in the end. Her eyes focussed on the message and she wasn't sure she could even blink.

*I was thinking somewhere … kid free.*

# Chapter 9

'So, you're *absolutely* sure you're okay to have them for the night?'

Brooke put Ollie down on the ground and he screeched, chasing Sugar back into the lounge room. Her … semi-date … with Lewis was that night—he'd suggested doing it the night of her day off. She supposed he figured she'd have more time to get ready that way and the kids wouldn't mind so much, considering she'd had the day with them.

'Of course, honey, but I'm just a little curious,' Lily said. 'I mean, I get minding them during the day, but it's very rare they have a sleepover.'

'Yeah, Brooke,' Georgie piped in, a mischievous smile on her face. 'What's going on?'

Brooke pressed her lips together, staring at her

sister. 'I just need a night to myself to … recover? It's been a very tiring week.'

'But they go to bed at seven, honey,' Lily said, her brow furrowed. 'Don't you get some you time after that?'

Brooke stared up at the ceiling, her nose crinkled. She'd wanted to tell her mother as little as possible, but she should have known there'd be questions if she was asking her to look after the kids on her day off. If her mother knew about Lewis, well, it would probably be over with before it could properly start. She didn't want to assume anything. She didn't want to say she and Lewis were something they weren't. Heck, she figured they were just two friends catching up. Getting to know each other. At a restaurant. In a date-like setting. *Shoot.*

'I'm not going to be at home,' she admitted, closing her eyes.

'Where will you be?' Georgie asked.

'Out.'

'With who?' Lily asked, her interest piquing.

'Oh, you know,' Brooke said, waving her hand awkwardly. 'With … friends.'

Georgie's eyebrow lifted. 'What friends?'

'Oh, just from … work.' What else was she supposed to say? It's not like she attended any playgroups or had any actual friends outside of work, and both her mother and sister knew that.

Georgie's other eyebrow joined her other and she rounded her mouth. She knew she was lying. *Shoot.* She knew she'd figure it out, but she really had no other excuse. She'd spent days trying to work out a good excuse and came up empty. She was already a terrible liar.

'Work,' Lily repeated, squinting, turning her focus on Georgie. 'Why aren't you going, then?'

Georgie lifted a finger. 'You know,' she said. '*That* is a good question.' Georgie stared at Brooke, her eyes wide.

Brooke felt her cheeks heating up. 'Well,' she said, drawing out the word. 'See … Georgie, umm, she …'

She snapped her mouth shut. She was going to have to confess, damn it. Otherwise, she'd lie herself into a ditch and her mother would either suss her out or deny looking after the kids until she told. And this was what she got for trying to do something. Bloody hell.

'I forgot,' Georgie said quickly.

'Hmm?' Brooke hummed, processing the lifeline her sister had given her.

'You … forgot?' Lily repeated, tilting her head a little.

Georgie nodded. 'Yep. I forgot. Silly me. Like Brooke said—big week.'

'So, are you going as well?' Lily said, placing her hands on her hips.

Georgie leaned a little more on the kitchen bench, her hand on her chin—since she was sitting on the bar stool. She looked more natural than Brooke could ever look in that position.

'I … guess I should,' Georgie said, glancing over at

Brooke. Brooke knew that look she was giving her. It was the *you owe me big* look she'd grown used to over the years. She'd also given that same look to Georgie at least as many times. 'But it seems I'll be running late, so you should go on ahead and I'll meet you there.'

'Oh,' Brooke said, her thoughts catching up to her. 'Oh, are you sure? I mean, I can … wait.'

Georgie slid off the bar stool gracefully. 'No, no,' she said, waving her hand. 'You go, have fun, I'll see you there.' She turned to head towards her room but stopped right before leaving the kitchen. 'Actually, before you do, can you help me pick something to wear?'

Brooke nodded, flashing a smile towards her mother—one she hoped was more convincing than it felt—and followed her sister. Once inside her room, Georgie pushed the door closed and put her hands on her hips.

'A *work* outing?' she hissed, loud enough only for Brooke to hear.

They'd spent a lot of time whispering about things in their rooms they didn't want their parents hearing. They'd found the perfect tone to use that could show as much emotion as needed without anyone outside their room being able to hear. Or, at least, that's what they thought. That's what Brooke hoped was still the case. Even if their parents *had* heard any of their chats, they'd never let in on the fact they knew. Brooke spread her arms out in surrender.

'What else could I say?' she said. 'She knows I don't have any other friends and I can hardly say I'm going on a date, can I?'

'Oh,' Georgie said, a knowing smile on her face. 'I *knew* it! It's with message guy, isn't it? Gladys's boy?'

'Lewis,' Brooke muttered. 'Yes, it is.'

'Lewis,' Georgie repeated, squinting. 'Well, I didn't actually know his name, but *cute*!'

Brooke rolled her eyes. 'I mean, I'm not sure if it's a *date* date, but we're having dinner.'

'Without the kids?' Georgie said, rummaging through her wardrobe. Brooke nodded. 'It's a date date, then.' She pulled a dress from her wardrobe and faced Brooke. 'I thought you said nothing was going to happen with you two.'

'It's not,' she muttered, folding her arms across her chest. 'I think we're just ... getting to know each other.'

Georgie's eyebrow lifted. 'You think?'

Brooke covered her face with her hands. 'I don't know, Georgie,' she groaned. 'He's a nice guy and ... good-looking. But neither of us are looking for anything and the kids keep wanting to have playdates so I—I don't know.' She looked back at Georgie to find her shrugging her dress on. 'Wait, you're not *actually* coming with, are you?'

'Oh, God, no,' Georgie said, pulling a disgusted face. 'I don't want to third-wheel whatever you're ... not ... having. It sounds boring.'

Brooke indicated to the dress. 'What are you doing, then?'

'Well, my dear sister,' Georgie said sarcastically. 'Thanks to you, I have to find something to do tonight that will keep me out late because I can't stay here.'

Brooke grimaced. 'Sorry,' she said. 'What are you going to do?'

Georgie shrugged. 'Probably go to Maia's and figure something out.' Her eyes widened. 'Maybe we'll get drunk and laugh about how you'll not be getting anything with your not-boyfriend on your not-date.'

'Oh, ha ha,' Brooke said, frowning. 'Laugh all you want, peach-face, but he's a nice guy.'

'I'm sure he is,' Georgie said, laughing.

Brooke turned to the door, but before she opened it, she turned back to her sister. 'And for your information,' she hissed, waggling her finger. 'Imperative is a totally normal word to use in casual conversation. I asked Lewis, and he agreed.'

Georgie laughed. 'You *asked* him? Well ... you're a wench!'

Brooke pressed her lips together. 'Correct usage, yes, but no. I am not a prostitute.'

Georgie's laugh increased. 'Oh, is *that* what it means?'

Brooke glared at her sister, smiled, and left. After all, she had a date to get to. Sort of.

***

Lewis checked the address on the message she'd

sent and looked at the number on the house again. Well, he had the right address, so it must be where she lived. It was one of the older houses in town and looked like a small, cute cottage—white weatherboard that looked in need of some paint, tin roof, and Victorian-style trims. He hadn't imagined her place would look like this, but if he thought about it, it suited her. He took a deep breath, tapping his hands on the steering wheel before unclipping his seatbelt and opening his door. He leaned to get out of the car and pulled himself back against the seat, closing the door.

What the hell was he doing? He couldn't go out with Brooke—certainly not as a proper date! He'd made a promise, and he was trying to make sure Gracie wouldn't get too attached. If things got serious with Brooke, then didn't work out, Gracie could get hurt. And he couldn't deal with that.

But it was too late now.

He was the fool who suggested they go out. He's the one that insisted on him picking her up instead of meeting her at the restaurant, so they would arrive at the same time, automatically making it more date-like than it might have been to start with. He's the one who hadn't been able to stop thinking about her since he met her, despite all his efforts.

He took another deep breath and glanced towards her house in time to see a curtain fall back into place in the window. She'd seen him. She knew he was here. It was way too late to change anything now, and he certainly didn't want her to think he was a coward by sitting in the car instead of going to her door. Even if he felt like one.

Swallowing the lump in his throat, he swung his door open again and jumped out, walking quickly to her door in hopes to get there before she did. He lifted his hand to knock, but before it could connect, the door swung open. Instinctively, he moved his hand to rub his jaw before dropping it to his side. She was dressed in dark blue jeans that hugged her legs in all the right places, and a dark off-the-shoulder shirt with large white flowers on it. Her hair was up in that high ponytail that gave him a good view of her slender neck and smooth shoulders. She was hopping on one foot as she slipped her second tanned high heel on. She was beautiful. And it took the breath out of him.

'Evening,' he said, feeling a little awkward.

'Hi! Oh, God,' she said nervously, losing her balance as she struggled with the clip on her high heel. Instinctively, he reached out, grabbing her arm to help her keep balance. Her arm was warm, and he felt the warmth pulse through his body. 'Thanks,' she said, finishing with the clip, and standing up straight.

He dropped his hands. 'I see you've got heels this time,' he said, indicating to her shoes.

'Hmm?' she hummed, grabbing her bag from the hall table. She looked down at her feet. 'Oh, right. Well, I didn't have someone else planning my outfit this time, for starters.' She moved out the door, closing it behind her and locking it. His eyes drifted to the nape of her neck and felt his breath catch. It looked soft, smooth, and he fought the urge to kiss her there. She turned to face him, and she took a shaky breath. 'Hi,' she said again, smiling.

He smiled back. 'Hi.'

There were only a few inches between them, it seemed. He could practically feel the warmth of her body reaching him. With heels on, her eyes were level with the tip of his nose, and when she lifted them to catch his gaze, they were a rich honey colour with a hint of umber. Her mouth opened slightly, but nothing came out. Then, she dropped her gaze, running her hands over her stomach.

'I hope this is okay,' she muttered. 'I'm not much of a dresses kind of girl. The one I wore at the party was my sister's.' She laughed shakily.

He took a few steps back, putting some distance between them. 'You look beautiful,' he said. 'And you did at the party, too, but it's okay if you don't like dresses.'

Her eyes widened. 'Oh, it's not that I don't *like* them,' she said. 'I just find them impractical—with the kids, I mean. I'd rather not bend down to pick Ollie up and have my panties on display.' She laughed awkwardly and bent her head. He was sure her cheeks had darkened. 'And *that* was too much information. Shall we?' She indicated towards the car.

He nodded, letting her lead the way, his eyes dropping to her ass and thighs that her jeans had on display. It seemed no matter how she dressed, she looked beautiful. He was sure she could wear a garbage bag and she'd still look gorgeous. And now, thanks to her comment, he couldn't help but wonder what *panties* she was wearing. *Damn it.*

Shaking his head to send his thoughts into more innocent territory, he jumped ahead of her to open the car door for her. Her cheeks darkened again, and she muttered a thank you. He took the long way around the car to his door, taking the moment to get his head sorted, and climbed into his seat. This wasn't a date. It couldn't be. They had to stay as friends. It was simply getting to know the person who his kid would apparently be spending a lot of time with. That's all.

So, why the hell couldn't he think of anything to say in the car while they drove to the restaurant? And why did she simply stare out her window, her hands twisted together, her knuckles white? And what colour *were* her panties?

He cleared his throat as he found a car park near the restaurant. 'So, I was thinking Italian,' he said, turning the car off.

'Italian sounds good,' she said, glancing at him with her smile.

He felt hotter but wasn't sure if it was him, the enclosed space, or the fact the air conditioner was no longer running since the car had stopped. He got out of the car and started walking around to the passenger side, but she'd already climbed out before he could get there. He locked the car once the door was closed and fell into step next to her, a foot or so between them.

'I was actually feeling like Italian today,' she said, crossing her arms over her chest, and staring at the pavement in front of them.

'What did you feel like?' he said. 'Pasta? Pizza?'

Her lips curved upwards, bearing her teeth. Even from a side-angle, she was beautiful. Heck, how was he going to do this? 'Pizza, actually,' she said, glancing up at him. 'I know, it's silly since we're going to a restaurant and not just a pizza place. But Italian restaurants make good pizzas.'

He nodded, smiling back. How could he not smile when she was smiling? He hooked his thumbs in the pockets of his jeans and nodded towards the restaurant he was taking her to. 'Well, this place does nice woodfired pizzas. And eggplant chips, too, if you want to give those a go.'

Her eyebrow lifted. 'Eggplant chips?'

'They're a whole lot nicer than they sound,' he said. 'Basically, like hot potato chips, except eggplant.'

She squinted. 'Do they go well with gravy? Because that's the only way I can eat hot chips.'

He feigned a grimace. 'I'm not sure gravy would go well with them,' he said. 'But they serve it with a lime aioli.'

She crinkled her nose. 'For the record, gravy goes well with everything,' she said. 'But I'll try your *eggplant* chips with their … aioli.' Her smile widened.

'*Lime* aioli,' he corrected.

She shook her head, her brow creased. 'What even is that?'

He held the door open for her. 'It's like … aioli … with lime juice and rind, I guess. I—' Her lips were pressed together, as though she was trying not to laugh, but the look in her eyes gave it away. 'Oh, you're *joking*.'

'Yes, I am,' she said, smirking. 'I've had lime aioli before, I know it's nice. Otherwise, I'd be asking for gravy.'

He laughed, shaking his head. She was a special kind of woman—in a good way. And one who's not afraid to admit she likes gravy, at that. Or to break the ice with a joke. He was just about certain every other woman at that party would have denied liking gravy. Heck, Alice wasn't even particularly fond of it, even though he loved it. In fact, that was something he liked about Brooke—that she spoke her mind. Had no filter, so to say. And said more than she intended to when she was obviously nervous, like how her sister had said she should get laid, and flashing her panties. *Damn*. How could he forget about that?

***

'Well?'

Brooke rolled her last bite of the eggplant chips around in her mouth, unable to drop the smile from her face. She'd been worried this … date … or whatever it was … would be awkward. And it seemed to start off that way—especially in the car. But by the time they'd got to the restaurant and started eating, it felt almost … natural. She swallowed her mouthful.

'Okay, I was a bit unsure about the first chip,' she admitted. 'But it sort of grows on you.'

He smiled—a brilliant natural smile that made her stomach flip. *Damn it*. How could she keep her feelings in check when he did that to her?

'I bet you'll be unable to resist them whenever you come here now,' he said, sipping his drink.

'You're probably right,' she sighed. 'If I ever came here again, of course.'

His smile dropped, and she wished she could have worded it differently. 'You didn't like the pizza?'

'Oh, no, the pizza was good,' she said quickly. 'Really nice actually. Everything was … nice.' *Including the company*. She could feel her cheeks heat up at the thought. She took a shaky breath, trying to find the words to say what she meant to say from the start. 'I meant if I ever get the chance again,' she said. 'I … I don't really … get out … much. You know, with the kids and everything.'

The smile crept back, though not as wide as it was before. He held her gaze, his eyes shifting side to side slightly as though searching her. 'Maybe we should do something about that,' he said, his tone deep, reaching her to her core.

Was he suggesting they make this a thing? Something flickered across his face she couldn't quite identify. He dropped his gaze to his hand, where he was fiddling with his napkin on the table. He shifted in his seat, and she realised his leg had been resting against hers. Her cheeks grew hotter, and her leg felt colder where his leg was no longer resting against. Why did it disappoint her that he'd moved?

'As friends, of course,' he said softly.

She stared at him, her breaths choppy. Why did that hurt? She'd already convinced herself they could only be friends—for the sake of the kids. So why did she hate that he said what she'd decided? He glanced up at her again and she realised his demeanour had changed completely. Weren't they having fun? Weren't they enjoying each other's company? So, why was his jaw set and his eyes looked more of a grey than the blue-green she'd dreamed about?

'Oh, this wasn't a … it was … friends,' she muttered. Why did she feel like a fool?

He nodded solemnly. 'I, umm,' he said, clearing his throat. 'I thought it would be a good idea to get to know each other more, since the girls are adamant on being best friends.'

'That they are,' she muttered, dropping her gaze to her empty plate.

What had made his demeanour change? Even if the date had started with him thinking they would just be friends, why had he changed? Why had he distanced himself? Wouldn't he have been the same the whole … not … date? They sat in silence for a moment and she kept her eyes on her plate, worried that if she caught his eye again, she might just start crying. Damn it, what had come over her? She put it down to exhaustion. She used to be level-headed, rarely cried, and always knew what was going on. Now, she was a sleep-deprived, stressed mother who couldn't see properly what was in front of her.

The waiter came over and took their plates and asked if they'd like to look at the dessert menu, but she stayed staring at the space where the plate had been. Why should he affect her this way? In all honesty, she was ready to go home and shut herself off for the night.

'Brooke?' She risked a glance up at Lewis. His brow was furrowed. 'Do you want dessert?' he said, his eyes didn't look as cold as they had before, and it only confused her more.

'N—no,' she croaked. 'I'm fine, thank you.'

She was worried that if she said any more, she might just break down. And she hated she felt that way. She knew they could only be friends, so his decision shouldn't bother her. But perhaps hearing him say it made it real. Had a small part of her wished it could have happened? Still, it shouldn't disappoint her like this, or make her wish she could run away. Damn him for insisting he picked her up!

'Shall we go then?' he said.

She nodded, rising out of her chair awkwardly and picking up her bag. She folded her arms across her chest and followed him towards the register. It wasn't until he'd already pulled out his card and paid for the meal that she realised she hadn't asked if they could split the bill. Surely *friends* shouldn't be in the habit of paying for each other. Not when it came to eating out at an actual restaurant. She dug around in her bag as he got the receipt and headed towards the door and pulled out her purse, grabbing enough cash out of her wallet to pay for roughly half of what they got. Once outside, she shoved it towards him, keeping her eyes on her outstretched hand instead of looking up at him.

'What's this for?' he said. He didn't take it.

'My share of the meal,' she said, wiggling her hand in a feeble attempt to make him take it. She could feel his gaze on her and felt her skin prickle. 'Take it, please.'

He was silent for a moment, but when he spoke, his voice was firm. 'No.'

She pressed her lips together, glancing up at him, surprised to find the blue returning to his eyes, even if it was dark and distant still. 'Please,' she said.

'No,' he repeated. 'It was my turn to pay.'

'For coffee,' she said. 'Not a meal out at a restaurant.'

He shrugged. 'Doesn't matter where it was, it was my turn.' He folded his hands over Brooke's outstretched one, but instead of taking the money, he pushed her hand closer to her body. 'Please, Brooke. Keep it. You can pay next time.'

He flashed a smile, his eyes flickering. But it only made her feel … gutted … instead of happy like it had before. He let go of her hand and started walking towards the car, her hand still pulsing where his had touched. Reluctantly, she stuffed the money back into her purse and followed him. He reached the car before her and held the door open. She stopped to face him before climbing in.

'We don't have to do this, Lewis,' she said quietly. He searched her with his eyes but didn't say anything. She shifted her gaze away from him, away from his car. 'This whole ... going out as friends ... thing. We can just have coffee when the girls have a playdate. We don't have to do ... this.'

She glanced back up at him and felt her breath catch. He was searching her, his brow creased, his expression almost ... pained. He opened his mouth, then closed it, taking a deep breath. God, she wished she could read his mind right now, see what he was thinking—whether or not he was just as confused about it all as she was. Whether or not he even *liked* her the same way she obviously liked him.

'I want to,' he said.

# Chapter 10

Why had he said that? Why had he said he only wanted to go out with her *as friends*? Bloody hell! That was the total opposite of what he'd been thinking about only moments before he said it! He'd been thinking about how natural it felt to be having dinner with her, having their legs resting against each other. How he'd wanted to reach out and put his hand on hers when she'd had it resting on the table while they waited for the food to come out, her fingers tapping in a slow rhythmic pattern on the table.

He'd wanted to twist their fingers together, see if her hand fit in his as perfectly as he'd imagined. He'd wanted to reach across the table and wipe the little speck of sauce from the corner of her lips, and he'd felt his stomach tighten when her tongue snuck out and delicately licked the speck away. He wanted to walk out of that restaurant hand in hand, or his arm around her bare shoulders. He wanted to know what damn colour her damn panties were!

Then, he thought of Alice. And Gracie. And his stupid brain took over his stupid mouth blurting out stupid things like wanting to be just friends. But as much as he hated it, it was probably for the best. Even if it looked like she was disappointed at it. But he still wasn't ready to just drop Brooke off at home and call it a night. No. He'd wanted to get to know her and he was damn well going to get to know her.

'Wh—what are your plans for the rest of the evening?' he said, risking a glance at her before pulling out of the car park.

She shrugged. 'Probably go for a little drive,' she muttered. 'Maybe watch a movie. I don't know. I'm not used to not having the kids at home.'

'Maybe we could drive around for a bit then,' he said hesitantly. 'Since we didn't really get much of a chance to talk over dinner.'

'If you want,' she said quietly.

*Damn.* This wasn't going to do. She was *clearly* disappointed about what he'd said, and it had done nothing in making their date less awkward. Heck, it made sure it *wasn't* a date. He wished he could go back in time and punch his past self in the face before he had a chance to say what he did. He had to save this ... somehow.

'You're stranded alone on a deserted island,' he

started. He flicked his eyes over to her to see she was looking at him surprised. He smiled, focussing back on the road, glad his plan already seemed to be working. 'You can have one thing—anything you want. What is it?'

'A book,' she said simply.

He glanced over at her. 'You're allowed to have anything you want, and you would take a book?'

'Well, it would be a good book,' she said. 'Like *The Swiss Family Robinson*, or something.'

He smiled. After years of using that as a conversation starter, he'd never once heard that as an answer. And it made more sense than any other responses he'd heard. 'That's practically a manual on surviving on a deserted island,' he said.

'Exactly,' she said. 'And it's an entertaining read. Unlike *actual* manuals.'

'Practical *and* entertaining.'

She smiled and seemed to relax in her seat. 'What would you choose?' she said.

'Well, I was going to say a boat or fresh water,' he said. 'But your idea makes a whole lot more sense. I'd never thought of it before.'

'Okay,' she said, shifting in her seat to face him better. 'You can be rich and lonely, or poor and happy. Which one are you?'

'Poor and happy,' he said without hesitation.

She made a sound as though she was almost shocked. 'But wouldn't you rather have money?'

He shrugged. 'You can always make do with what you have,' he said. 'Haven't you heard of living within your means? Besides, what's the point of having money if you've got no one to share it with?'

'I guess so,' she said.

'You'd rather the money?'

'Not really,' she said. 'But I wouldn't mind a happy medium.'

He smiled, taking a turn towards Pethard Place Lookout—otherwise known as Mickey Mouse Hills. 'But that wasn't one of the options,' he pointed out.

She hesitated for a moment, and when he glanced over at her, she was looking at him, smiling. It spread a warmth through him, and he found himself wishing again he hadn't mentioned the friends thing.

'Well, in that case,' she said, sighing, looking out the windscreen instead of at him. 'I would choose poor and happy. I suppose I'd be all right having no money—since I'd be happy, and all.'

He laughed, angling the car to get a good view at the top of the lookout and pulling it to a stop. He heard her sigh and wondered if it sounded a little shaky. He turned in his seat slightly to face her better. She seemed more relaxed in her seat now, at least compared to when he picked her up and especially compared to when they got back into the car. She was focussed on the view. The sun was still setting—one of the joys of daylight saving time— sending an orange hue over their view of Bendigo.

'It's beautiful,' she said, breathlessly.

'It is,' he said. But he wasn't looking at the view.

She turned her head to face him, and for a split

second, she looked real. Raw. Almost … vulnerable. And comfortable. Her lips parted slightly, and he was sure he'd heard a sharp intake of breath. He swallowed the lump in his throat and shifted his gaze to the view in front of them, seemingly not as good as the one he was just looking at. But he couldn't let himself go there. And he'd made it clear to her over dinner. Even if he wished he hadn't.

'Favourite soup?' he said, forcing himself not to look at her.

'Bought, or homemade?'

'Both.'

'Crab and sweetcorn for bought,' she said. 'Egg drop soup for homemade. You?'

'Chicken and sweetcorn,' he said. 'And Moroccan sweet potato, carrot, and chickpea for homemade.'

'Chicken and sweetcorn is your favourite bought soup?' she repeated. 'But it's so easy to make!'

He smiled, glancing at her amused expression. 'I know,' he said. 'But they somehow make it a better consistency than I can.'

She laughed. 'Well, I'm not going to argue with that,' she said. 'It must be their secret ingredient.'

He felt himself relax, relieved it wasn't feeling awkward between them anymore. 'Must be,' he said.

She looked back out at the view, her smile wide. 'Okay,' she said, thoughtfully. 'Sweet or savoury?'

'Savoury,' he said, tilting his head to the side. 'Unless it's ice cream. You?'

'Savoury,' she agreed. 'Mostly. But I sometimes feel like sweet, and if I do, then it's *all* the sweets.'

'No holds barred?' he teased.

'I will send myself into a sugar coma,' she laughed. 'And suffer from a sugar hangover the next day. But then I'm back on savoury for a while.'

He chuckled. 'You are an interesting woman, Brooke. Do you know that?'

She crinkled her nose, glancing back at him for just a brief moment. 'I had my suspicions.'

'Do dream jobs exist?' he asked.

'Honestly?' she said. 'I don't think so. I think it's all romanticised and we think it could be our dream job. But what's to say we're not going to like it? I don't think a dream job is what everyone thinks it is.'

'What do you think it is?'

She shrugged, picking at a spot on her jeans. 'I think it sneaks up on you. It's surprising. In my opinion, a dream job is a job you can be content with—that you can see yourself working there for many years.'

'Are you in your dream job?'

She bit her lower lip. 'I don't think I'll be going anywhere,' she said. 'It's a better workplace than most.' She took a deep breath, then looked up at him again. 'I used to want to be a teacher, you know.'

He bit the inside of his cheek. Was being a teacher her dream job? Had she just hit a dangerous level of content with her workplace that she thought being a teacher was unattainable? 'What happened?' he said hesitantly.

Something flickered in her eyes—something resembling amusement and a hint of that teasing she'd had when she made the joke about gravy. 'I had kids,' she said, her lips curving to one side. 'And I decided there was no way in hell I was going to subject myself to lots of other people's kids by choice.'

'But it would be different,' he said. 'They'd be older than yours are now.'

She shrugged one shoulder, and he was certain her shirt had dropped a little lower, making his stomach tie in a knot. 'I love my kids,' she said, tilting her head to the side, and exposing the delicate part of her neck. *Damn it.* 'But I can barely stand them half the time. And I know I've got it relatively easy compared to other people. I mean, they have no allergies and they're perfectly healthy kids. They just … test me. I couldn't deal with a class full of kids that also want to test me.'

'And you're not just settling for the job you have?'

Her eyebrows pulled together as she studied him. 'I like my job,' she said. 'I get enough hours, it pays well enough, and the person that annoys me most is my sister.'

'Well, that's saying something,' he teased.

She laughed, the sound pulsing through him in a glorious manner. 'Yes, it is,' she said, nodding. 'What about you? Did you always want to be a building contractor?'

'I did, actually,' he said, laughing. 'So, I guess you could say I got my dream job. It's equally frustrating and enjoyable—just as I'd imagined.'

'Well, good for you,' she said, nudging his shoulder with her hand. 'You deserve to have your dream job.'

They grew silent for a moment, watching as the sun ducked behind the hills, suspending them in darkness. He could still see her faintly in the greyness of dusk, and they watched as the lights of the town became more obvious than they were while the sun was setting.

'What are your ... thoughts,' he started, staring at the lights. 'On soul mates?'

She stayed silent for a moment, and he wondered why that would be the next get-to-know-you question he asked. Out of the corner of his eye, he saw her drop her head, her hands clasped together. She was running her left thumb over her right thumbnail.

'I think there's one person out there for everyone,' she said quietly. 'And that it's possible to feel like you're in love with someone who's not necessarily the right person. At the time, it's easy enough to mistake them as the right one, but it might turn out otherwise.'

'How do you know if they're the right one or not?' he said, hesitantly.

She laughed. 'How should I know?' she said. 'You're the one that's been married, what do you think?'

He shrugged, taking a deep breath. 'I guess it's one of those things you just know when it happens,' he said.

She nodded. 'And suddenly, it's obvious that everything else wasn't right,' she finished.

'Is that how it felt with you and Brett?' he asked, hoping his question wouldn't push her away. 'That he was right for you?'

She exhaled, resting her head back against the headrest. She tilted her head slightly towards him, a weary smile on her face. 'I didn't marry him, did I?' she said, returning her gaze towards the lights of the town. 'I'm not sure I ever felt he was *the* guy,' she continued. 'But there were a lot of things that felt right at the time. It only started to go wrong after I was already pregnant.'

'Is there more to the story?'

She dropped her gaze to her hands again, her shoulders stiffening. 'I really don't want to talk about him,' she said. 'If you don't mind.'

'Sure,' he said. 'Would you ever consider marrying someone now? If he was the right guy?'

She shrugged again. 'If I knew he was the right guy, sure,' she said. 'But I have a lot more to think about now. It's not just me anymore. What about you? Do you think you'd marry again?'

He felt his body tense and his lips pressed together. What did he expect? He'd asked her, why shouldn't she ask him back? After all, he didn't know what the hell to think anymore.

***

Even in the darkness, she could see him tense. Was it

a sorer topic for him than it was for her? Truth is, with Brett, she'd known she would never marry him. She'd known he might not have been the *right* guy for her. But she hadn't expected anything to be permanent with him. Then, she had Maddie. And it was too late for it to not be permanent because she would always have a child to remind her of what she had with Brett. And, for a while, things were okay with him. They weren't *great*, but they were okay. Then, it got too much when she fell pregnant again and all the skeletons came out of the closet.

It had been a hard time for her. And for so long, she'd never thought she'd ever marry or find another man. After all, it wasn't easy to find a guy who was willing to take on a woman with kids. If she found a man who was willing to do that, she'd want him to treat her kids as his own. Especially since their biological father seemingly wanted nothing to do with them. And *that* would be harder to find. Though, she couldn't help but think Lewis was that kind of guy. Her mind flicked back to their playdate at the trampoline place, when he took Ollie for a while. He'd seemed so natural, and he was so good with him.

But it wasn't to be. He'd made that clear before. But maybe he'd still be a father figure for the kids, even if they were just friends. And she would be happy with that. Even if she was still lonely.

'I ... didn't ... think I would,' he said slowly, snapping her thoughts to the present. 'I thought she was the one for me, that there wouldn't be anyone else. I figured I'd only be married once, you know? But I never thought she'd … she…' He took a shaky breath, and she felt a fist clenching in her chest. 'I don't know anymore, Brooke. I can't help … thinking … wondering … if she really was the one for me. And if she was, why was she taken so soon?'

She could feel her eyes burning, and her throat tightening. At least with Brett, she knew. Lewis would never know—not really. He'd still been in love with Alice when he lost her. Brooke had time to realise she was never in love with Brett as much as she'd thought. She couldn't imagine how Lewis might be feeling. God, even if he hadn't mentioned he wanted to stay friends with her, she still would have had no right to even think about anything with him.

'I—I'm sorry,' she muttered, wiping her eyes in an attempt to hide the tears. He was staring out at the lights, his jaw set, his Adam's apple bobbing up and down as he swallowed.

'I can barely see her anymore,' he said, his voice low, filled with something she couldn't quite place. 'It's like her memory is slowly fading and all I see is—'

He broke off, bringing his gaze to hers, his eyes dark—even in the darkness around them, she could see it. She swallowed the lump in her throat, blinking back the tears. What did he see? She couldn't ask him. She could never ask him to finish that sentence because she felt it would be either dangerously close to the more-than-friends line or break her heart. And she wasn't sure how the first would make her feel.

'It's okay,' she whispered, pushing a smile onto her face, even if it felt fake. 'We don't have to talk about it.'

He nodded slowly but remained quiet. She dropped her gaze to her hands, sure she'd just about rubbed her thumbnail off over the course of the night. She could feel his gaze resting on her, and it made her hairs stand on end and a warmth spread through her stomach. After a moment, he started up the car and they were on their way again—to her home, she supposed. There weren't many other places their conversation could go after something as intense as that.

She relaxed into the chair as much as she could and tried to sort out her thoughts and confusion. Why had he asked if she believed in soul mates? Was it simply something that had been bothering him, since he'd been finding it harder to remember Alice? Or was it something else? Sure, it was something she'd been thinking about lately. Since meeting Lewis, to be exact. But she'd never had much incentive or inspiration for the thought to even cross her mind before that.

Then, her thoughts drifted to all the what ifs she could think of. What if things were different—could they have worked? What if they didn't have the common ground of having kids that liked to spend time together? What if they could move past their insecurities and work it out? Would they last?

He was such a nice guy, and the kind of guy she could fall for—and she would fall hard. Heck, she was worried it had already started. He was handsome—attractive in so many ways—kind, funny, sweet. He had his antics that made her smile.

'You call her *noodle*.' It took her a second to realise she'd spoken out loud, rather than thinking it.

'Gracie?' he said. She nodded, then realised he might not have seen it.

'Yes, Gracie,' she said. 'You call her *noodle*. Is there a story behind that?'

In the flashes of light from the streetlights, she could see the smile creep back onto his face, his expression softening. It made her heart skip a beat. Did she mention he was attractive? Because with the light hitting him like this, attractive would be a total understatement.

'Nothing too exciting,' he said. 'She went through a stage where she refused to eat just about anything but noodles. So, I started calling her noodle and I guess it stuck.'

'Huh,' she hummed. 'I thought there must be a story with it.'

He glanced over at her for a split second, smiling, then turned into her street. 'Don't you have pet names for your kids?'

She smiled, hesitating a moment. 'Nugget,' she said. 'For Maddie. And, well, Ollie gets Matey most of the time. But I have no idea where they came from. I think I just came out with them one day and kept on with it.'

He laughed. 'And you were asking me if there was a story behind my pet name for her?'

She felt her cheeks heat up as he pulled the car to a stop. 'I know, I'm a bit of a hypocrite.'

'Not at all,' he said, opening his door.

She took a deep breath once he was out of the car, partly relieved their not-date was almost over, but also a little disappointed at the same time. She opened the door but found it opened quicker than she'd intended. It was then she realised he was at her door and had opened it for her, which confused her even more. Sure, he'd opened her door when she got in the car. But was *that* even a friend thing to do? She wouldn't know. She'd never really experienced time with a gentleman.

Brett had never been one for opening doors for her. Or really doing anything for her, for that matter. He was all for equality, which included doing everything herself and then some, which she later realised wasn't equality—it was just him being lazy.

With Lewis acting like a gentleman, opening doors for her, paying for her meal—even if he claimed she could pay next time. The way he acted at the shops, looking after her, in a way, by letting her sit while he got the coffee and food. The way he took care of Ollie, so she could have her hands free at the trampoline place. Why hadn't she fully registered it before? Lewis was totally different to Brett, in possibly every way. And the weird feeling in her stomach when she was around him had to be something different to just nerves, regardless of what she'd been telling herself.

She climbed out of the car and he closed the

door, then indicated towards her house. God, he was even going to walk her to her door! What was she supposed to do? What did one do in this kind of situation? It was the first time she was really experiencing it, so she had no idea. Slowly, she eased towards her front door, fully aware of him walking closely behind her. By the time they reached the door, her mind was in full swing and her breathing shallow. Should she invite him in for a cup of tea? Something stronger? Show him around the house?

She had *no* idea how the not-really-but-sort-of date went. Sure, they'd got to know each other a little better, and despite him making it clear he wanted to just be friends with her, they hit some very intense topics that didn't seem like the kind of thing normal friends who are getting to know each other talk about. And she couldn't shake the thought that maybe—*maybe*—things had changed again after he said the friends thing. And it could have quite possibly changed to something more serious.

She took as deep a breath as she could, unlocking the door, but she didn't open it. Not yet. She turned to face him, surprised to find he was standing closer than she'd thought. His expression was troubled, and she wondered if his mind was having the same battle that hers was. But in his eyes was something else. His eyes were darker, but not cold. Intense. And they were searching hers.

'I, umm,' she muttered, attempting to drop her gaze, but failing. It's as though his gaze was holding her captive and she couldn't escape it. Nor did she want to. 'I enjoyed tonight. Thank you.'

He nodded slightly—so slightly she almost missed it. And she wasn't prepared for how deep his voice sounded when he spoke. 'Tell me we'll do it again,' he said.

It wasn't a question. It was soft, low, but also partly … firm … as though it was laced with something she hadn't noticed there before. Something that made her insides come alive and her heart start pounding in her chest. It was quiet around them, and she was almost convinced he could hear her heart pounding as much as she could.

She lived on a quiet street—one that mostly only had the street-dwellers going past. But tonight, it was almost quieter than usual. That, or the intensity in his eyes drowned out every other sound. His hand lifted, and he swept her fringe away from her eyes, making her breath catch, his fingertips lingering. She felt her lip quiver slightly, a feeling she was not used to, especially when it had nothing to do with crying.

She nodded, unable to find the words—any words—to say. His brow furrowed, and his fingertips travelled down the side of her face to her chin, then the backs of his fingers eased across her jawline, sending another sensation she wasn't used to shooting through her body. She was glad it was dark, because she had to rest slightly against the door to keep upright, and she hoped he couldn't tell.

'Promise me,' he said again, his tone deeper, almost like a growl. A growl that sent a shiver down her spine.

Promise what, exactly? Promise they'd go out again *as friends*? Or promise it would be something else? Because having him touch her like this—his hand sneaking around to cup the back of her neck— and feeling the way she did was something completely out of the realm of friendship.

'I promise,' she whispered.

The words had barely escaped her mouth when his lips were on hers and any breath she still had left her body. He kissed her hard, fervently, but somehow gently at the same time. And his thumb caressed the side of her neck, sending a pulse all the way to her core. Any thought that had been rolling around in her head had vanished. Any sound, sensation—everything had been forgotten about, and it was just her and Lewis and the sensations he made her feel.

The way his mouth tasted entirely different to anything she'd ever had before, and the only way to describe it was that all she was tasting was uniquely him. Masculine, passionate, tempting, addictive. Him. Her tongue danced with his rhythmically, connecting them on another level. And his cologne was stronger than she'd registered earlier, which possibly had something to do with the fact their bodies were pressed against each other. His other hand pressed against her lower back, and she dove her own hands into his hair, deepening the kiss. His kisses, taste, smell, and sensations she felt made for a heady combination and she somehow felt ... drunk. On him, on the moment, she wasn't sure. But she was sure she didn't want to be just friends with him. She wanted so much more.

She reached a hand behind her and felt for the doorknob, relieved when she found it, and pushed the door open, taking a step back, pulling him with her. But he didn't budge. In fact, he felt as though his body stiffened, and the warmth she'd been feeling, the passion, dissipated.

'Lewis,' she whispered, breaking the kiss. Didn't he want it, too? Wasn't *that* kiss proof of it?'

He released her as though his hands had just been shocked, and in the brief second her eyes searched his before he turned, putting some distance between them, she noticed the look had changed. Again. He wasn't looking at her with that certainty, that desire and passion she'd seen before the kiss. They were wide, troubled. Regretful. It gutted her.

He groaned, running one hand through his hair, his other hand clutching to the railing of her porch. She folded her arms across her chest and pressed her lips together, trying not to feel the pain of rejection, trying to hold back the tears. But it was pointless. She dropped her gaze, swallowing the lump in her throat. She hadn't wanted it to become like this. She'd decided they could only be friends, and he'd obviously thought the same. Then, somehow, it changed. And now? Now she didn't know what to think.

'I'm sorry,' he said quietly, his back still towards her. His tone was still deep, though somehow different to before. 'I shouldn't have ... done ... that.'

He took a deep breath—she could tell by the way his firm shoulders lifted and fell. Then, he seemed to straighten up and, slowly, turned to face her. She hoped it was too dark for him to read her face. Her eyes would surely have been puffy since they burned from the threat of unshed tears. And he would have been able to see it if she even had the slightest bit of light on her. She hoped her face was in the shadow, rather than where the streetlight next door hit. But she suspected he saw, since his expression turned more apologetic.

'Brooke,' he said, taking a step forward.

Instinctively, she took a step back, feeling her heart drop as she did. He froze in place, his shoulders dropping a little more, a look crossing over his face that could easily be taken as hurt. But what did it matter, really? It was clear how it was going to play out. And it was probably just as well it was happening now before it got too far.

'G—goodnight, Lewis,' she muttered, shifting her head to look away from him—*beyond* him. Towards his car, specifically.

He didn't move for a moment, and she wondered what he was thinking about—whether he regretted everything to do with her. Regretted talking to her in the shops when he could have pretended like he didn't recognise her. Regretted going on a playdate with her at the trampoline place and making her promise to see him again. Where did that all stand, now?

Finally, after what seemed like forever of silence,

he nodded. 'Goodnight, Brooke,' he said quietly.

Then, he left, taking only a second to glance back at her before he climbed into his car. He almost smiled. She was sure she'd seen his lips flick up slightly to one side before it was replaced with his hardened, distant look. It wasn't until she'd retreated inside that she *really* noticed how weak her knees were and exactly how close she was to tears. She closed the front door, sinking to the ground, leaning against it. Her kids' room was empty. Heck, her whole house was empty. She was alone, with no one but herself to mourn for what she'd almost had, wondering what the hell happened to make it such a rollercoaster night.

# Chapter 11

He was a mess.

He'd had one thing he'd been so sure of, and he'd blown it away with one fell swoop. Why did he kiss Brooke? Well, he knew *why*. Because he couldn't resist her—not for another second—and couldn't stand the thought of not seeing her again. And it was totally irrational of him. Irrational and irresponsible. Like everything he did that involved her.

But it was the only thing that made sense.

The way he couldn't get her out of his head, the way her smile made him want to wrap her up in his arms and kiss her senseless. The way it was easy with her. Easy to smile when she smiled, easy to talk to her about anything—*anything*—and easy to feel things for her he hadn't felt in a very long time. No, it was different. He loved Alice. He married Alice. He'd started a life with Alice. And yet, these feelings for Brooke were both similar and somehow different to those he felt for Alice. And it terrified him.

Why shouldn't it? He'd thought he'd never feel anything for anyone else ever again. He'd thought he would always be the widower with a kid who hid from society and didn't talk to people if he could avoid it. Who spent his days and nights feeling lonely and mourning after his dead wife.

Then he kissed Brooke. And none of what he'd previously accepted made sense. She made sense. And he couldn't chase it. He couldn't chase her. He'd been more into that kiss than he should have been—*so* close to losing the tiny bit of control he still had. Too close to taking it too far and ruining what could have been a good friendship. Or maybe it was already too late for that.

Why would she want to see him again after he ran off like that?

How could he expect her to *want* to go back to being friends after that? How could *he* go back to being friends? He didn't know anymore. All he knew was he barely made it through the past twenty-four hours knowing he might have screwed everything up.

'Lewis, you in there, son?'

He blinked back to the present to see Alice's parents—Gerald and Eve Meller—facing him, concerned. As had become tradition, he'd brought Gracie over to her grandparents' place for Thursday night dinner. It was the least he could do. And it had been hard at first when they were still getting used to not having Alice there. But with time, he'd grown used to it. He stared at his empty plate, his hands still clutching his knife and fork.

'You're miles away, Lewis,' Eve said.

'What's going on in that old think tank of yours?' Gerald said.

He shook his head slowly, placing his cutlery on his plate. 'Just had a bit going on,' he said. The last thing he wanted was to tell them what he was *actually* thinking about. It'd be like telling them he didn't love Alice anymore.

Gracie let out a loud sigh next to him, clattering her fork onto her plate. 'He's thinking about Brooke, duh,' she said, resting her head back against her chair.

He felt his jaw clench instinctively, his body heating up. He should have figured Gracie was going to blurt it out. Then again, he hadn't exactly thought she would know that much about it. Alice's parents looked at him in a way he couldn't quite discern.

'Brooke, hmm?' Gerald said, stabbing his fork into his last bite of steak, and popping it in his mouth. 'Who's that?'

'She's, umm,' he stammered.

'She's my best friend's mummy,' Gracie piped in, leaning on the edge of her chair. She would likely fall off if she was just a fraction closer to the edge. He'd grown used to not worrying about it too much if it wasn't going to hurt her badly. 'She's *really* pretty and *really* nice.'

'Gracie,' he warned.

'And Daddy likes her, don't you Daddy?' she said, flicking her big brown eyes up towards him. *Oh, boy.*

'What makes you say that, noodle?' he said, focussing on her.

'Because I like her,' she said, frowning. 'And you spend an *awful* lot of time with her.'

'We've been on a couple of playdates—for the kids,' he said to Gerald and Eve, his heart racing. This kid was going to expose him and break her grandparents' hearts. He briefly considered giving her chair a little bump to see *how* close to falling off she was, then decided against it.

'Well, we *have*,' Gracie continued, oblivious of the warning in Lewis's eyes. 'But you had dinner with her last night and I had to stay with Nanna. You told me not to say anything to her, but I'm allowed to tell Gran and Grandpa, aren't I?'

He pressed his lips together and leaned in close. 'Why don't you go finish watching your movie for a while, hmm?' he said.

Gracie's shoulders dropped. 'But Gran says—'

'It's all right, sweetie,' Eve said. 'You can watch it.'

Gracie's mouth widened into a toothy grin and she slid off her chair, her curls bouncing as she raced towards the television. He took a deep breath and faced his in-laws.

'So,' Gerald said, clearing his throat. 'Dinner, huh?'

'As friends,' he said, defensively. 'Nothing more

than … friends.'

They both stared at him for a moment that seemed to drag on, then Eve let out a big sigh. 'Oh, Lewis, you've always been a terrible liar,' she said, shaking her head, her brow furrowed. 'That's one of the things our Alice saw in you.'

'She saw a lot in you,' Gerald said. 'Your honesty, loyalty.'

'Perhaps too loyal,' Eve finished.

He frowned. 'What do you mean?'

'Do you like her, Lewis?' Eve said.

'I loved Alice,' he said.

'Brooke,' Gerald said. 'She's talking about Brooke.'

'I wouldn't do that to Alice,' he said, he suspected more to convince himself than her parents. 'I married Alice, I wouldn't do that to her.'

'Well, I'd hope not,' Eve said. 'If things were different.' She sighed, dropping her gaze to her empty plate. 'If she was still here.'

'But I'd also say she would want you to be happy,' Gerald said.

'She was always like that,' Eve continued, growing distant, her eyes glistening. 'Always putting those she loved ahead of herself.'

'She was very selfless,' Lewis added.

'Which is why we were on board with the party,' Gerald said.

Lewis's eyes widened. 'The party?' he repeated. He'd thought they didn't know! That it was solely his meddling mother's doing.

'Yes, the party Gladys threw for you,' Eve said, waving her hand towards him. She was back in the present again. 'We agreed it would be a good idea to try setting you up with someone, you know, for Gracie's sake. Oh, she needs a mother, Lewis.'

'She has a mother,' he said flatly, though he found the conviction he'd had all this time was no longer there.

'We're not saying you'll be replacing Alice,' Gerald said, rubbing his forehead. 'You've already done a good job of making sure Gracie knows who her mother is, and we appreciate that. But we also acknowledge that having another woman in your lives who she can have a mother-daughter relationship with will be a benefit for both of you.'

Lewis pinched the bridge of his nose with his thumb and forefinger. 'So, you both knew about the party and didn't *tell* me?'

Gerald and Eve shared a look. 'We knew you wouldn't go if you knew,' Eve said softly.

'You're right, I wouldn't have,' he said. 'I am capable of finding someone on my own.'

'It's been five years,' Gerald said.

'I needed time,' he said.

'We understand that, but—' Eve started.

'Eve wants more grandchildren, Lewis,' Gerald said, fiddling with the edge of his plate.

Lewis's eyebrow shot up. 'You do realise they wouldn't be blood-related, right?'

'Of course we know that,' Eve said as though he was stating the obvious. 'But you're a son to us, and we would treat any one of your children—blood-related or not—as our grandchildren. But what we're trying to say is we want you to be happy. Alice would want you to be happy. And even though you've been coping for five years. Can you honestly say you've been happy?'

He traced his fingertips along the pattern on the tablecloth. How could he have been happy? The only reason why he could have been truly happy over the last five years had been taken from him. Sure, Gracie made him happy, and he loved her so much. But it wasn't the same as having someone to share your life with. Share your bed with.

'We don't want you avoiding relationships because of us,' Gerald said. 'So, if it's this Brooke, or if it's someone else, go for it, son.'

'So, tell me,' Eve said, clearing her throat. 'Is she pretty?'

He studied them for a moment. What they said made sense. They had always treated him like a son, especially after Alice died. Alice had been an only child, and he'd been more than happy to fill the son slot in their family. He also knew Alice would want him to be happy. She'd want him to move on, especially if it would benefit Gracie. And maybe he'd just been fighting to accept that for the last five years. Or maybe he was just waiting for the right time. The right person.

He smiled, nodding slowly. 'Very.'

***

It was a normal Friday. Exactly the same as every other Friday. She'd wake up, have breakfast, get the kids ready, take them to her parents' place, go to work, and go through the normal processes of the day. It was routine. Nothing out of the ordinary. Except the time was going so damn slowly, and she was not feeling it one bit.

It couldn't just be the day—once every so often where the day is just a below-average day— especially since yesterday was the same. Slow. Agonisingly slow. And she knew why.

Lewis.

And that kiss.

That damned kiss that broke down her barrier then made him freak out like that. She hadn't heard from him since, and it was slowly killing her, she was sure of it. Why did he freak out? Was that kiss not as incredible for him as it was for her? In those moments, where his lips were on hers and her body was pressed against his, she saw it all. She saw what their future could look like, what made him different to any other guy. Why it would work with him where it didn't with Brett. And then, in an instant, it was gone.

Gone, because he didn't want it. Because he broke away, *apologised* for kissing her, making it clear once again he didn't want that. Well, neither had she. At least, she'd thought she hadn't wanted it. But now? Now, she didn't know what to *really* think. She didn't know what she wanted. Then again, she had a feeling she did. She wanted him. She just didn't *want* to want him.

She touched her fingers to her lips where she could still feel his kiss lingering, even though two nights had passed, and she still hadn't heard from him. Not even a message. Then again, she could message him, too. But what would she say? She wasn't even sure he wanted to see her again, let alone talk to her. Or how it would even go—how she would cope with the idea of going back to being friends with him, knowing how incredible it made her feel when he kissed her.

*Damn it*.

Damn it all! Damn him. Damn their meddling mothers. Damn her, for letting herself actually *feel* like this for the guy. She'd had an existence she'd been content with. It worked. Now, she wasn't content. It wasn't working. She wanted more. And she couldn't have it.

She blinked back her thoughts, focussing on bagging the jewellery she'd just finished cleaning. These tasks had once succeeded in distracting her, keeping her hands busy enough to forget about the fact she was raising her kids alone. That she had to work hard just to survive. But now, it all seemed menial. And it did nothing to distract her. She stretched her arms up above her head, leaning back to work the kink out of her back. That was another thing she could blame Lewis for, since sleep hadn't come easy for her because of him. Her ears pricked up when she heard a deep voice, followed by her sister's smooth talking.

She couldn't make sense of the words, but she suspected she might have known the voice, especially since her sister wasn't talking the same way she usually would when talking about jewellery. Surely, not. It couldn't be him, could it? She had to be imagining it. It was nothing but her stupid mind playing stupid tricks on her.

She'd almost convinced herself of it when Georgie came into the back room, a concerned look on her face. 'There's someone here to see you,' she said. 'Tall, dark hair, sexy, and *gorgeous* eyes. Are you talking to him?'

God, it *was* him. She couldn't think of any other guy who would fit Georgie's description. Heck, even if she simply said there was a guy here to see her, she would have known. She shook her head slowly, feeling her chest tighten. Why was he here? Why did he want to see her now, when he could have sent her a message? Why would he be visiting her at work when he knew where she lived?

'We haven't since the … dinner,' she mumbled.

'Do you want to talk to him?'

'I—I don't know.'

'I'll take that as a no,' Georgie said. 'Don't worry, I'll send him on his way.'

Before Brooke could sort her thoughts out, Georgie had already gone out the front. She could hear the mumbling, then his voice was louder.

'Is she back there? Brooke!'

She felt her skin prickle. Should she talk to him?

She didn't know what to say! And she certainly hadn't thought about what he *might* say and how she would respond. Should she slap him for running out on her? Should she simply hear what he has to say and take it like a grown woman? She would have felt a whole lot better if she felt like she had a choice in anything, if she hadn't been frozen in place.

'Hey, you can't be back here!' Georgie yelled, her voice higher-pitched than normal.

'I just need to talk to her,' he said, firmly.

Before she knew it, he'd pushed his way into the back room and stared at her, a mixture of shock and apprehension crossing his face. Or maybe it was simply mirroring hers.

'Does Gladys know you're here?' Georgie said, sulkily, placing her hands on her hips.

'Georgie, it's fine,' Brooke mumbled.

Lewis's eyes widened as he turned to Georgie. 'Oh, so *you're* her sister?'

Georgie lifted her chin, squinting. 'Yes, I am.'

'So, you'll understand why I need to talk to her, then.'

'Because you're a—'

'*Georgie*!' Brooke said firmly.

'What?'

'It's fine,' she said. 'He won't be long, I'm sure.'

Georgie glanced between the two of them, then huffed, storming out to the front room. She couldn't resist her lips curving up a little at her sister's attitude. She took a deep breath, suddenly feeling like the back room was much smaller than it actually was, especially with him standing there with his eyes on her. She turned her attention towards him. His mouth opened, then closed, then opened again, but nothing came out. His hands were by his side, alternating between clenching and stretching. Well, she wouldn't talk first. He's the one that wanted to talk, so he could be her guest. Her eyebrow lifted, and she pressed her lips together.

'Hey,' he said, finally, softly. He took a step closer, and she felt her body tense. He halted, looking around the room awkwardly.

'Hi,' she said, flatly.

'I, umm,' he stammered. 'I've been … thinking … about our, umm, what happened the other night.'

She leaned back, resting against the bench behind her, her hands planted firmly on it to keep herself upright. She kept her mouth shut. What could she say? That she hadn't stopped thinking about it? That it had been driving her insane the last two days, and she'd been working very hard to try to get herself out of that funk? That numbness?

'I get that you might be mad at me,' he said, shifting his weight to one side as though he'd considered moving towards her then decided against it. 'And you have every right to be. I freaked out, and I ran away. And I shouldn't have.'

Certain that her lower back resting against the bench would keep her upright, she folded her arms across her chest, dropping her gaze, though keeping her head straight. She bit into her lip to stop herself from saying anything she'd regret. She needed him to keep talking. She needed him to say everything he'd wanted to say before she said anything.

'I haven't … been … with anyone,' he said. 'Since Alice. I haven't had any kind of relations with a woman, or even a friendship, for that matter. I didn't even … want … it.'

Her eyes started to burn, and she blinked a few times to keep the tears from falling. She could feel her body heating up, and she felt as raw as she had after his kiss. Is that what he came here for? To remind her of everything he'd already told her? He didn't want a relationship—he'd made that clear from the start. He wanted to only be friends, playdates with the kids, nothing more. And it had been exactly what she'd wanted.

'Until now,' he said, taking a shaky breath. She lifted her gaze slowly to meet his. There was something in his eyes—a something that reminded her of the same something that had been there before he'd kissed her. 'I thought I didn't want any of that,' he continued. 'I'd convinced myself Alice was it for me, and that was that. But then I met you, and none of what I'd told myself really made sense anymore. I can't just be friends with you. It's more than that.'

She felt her breath suck into her lungs but didn't feel it leave. Her lips parted, quivered, even, and she swiped at her eyes to keep the tears from falling, though she was sure they probably looked puffy by now. He took a step closer—a small step—and she was surprised she didn't tense up or move instinctively. She couldn't let herself feel like this. If he ran off on her after kissing her, what's to say he wouldn't run off when things got hard? She couldn't just let herself fall back into his arms if he said a few smooth words to her. She'd done that with Brett, and she wouldn't do it again.

'Brooke, please say something,' he pleaded. 'I'm not used to talking this much without a response. Or at all, for that matter, not like this.'

She swallowed the lump in her throat, studying him. His eyes were pleading, too. They were warm, worried, and somehow distant as if holding back. She took a shaky breath, opening her mouth to speak, worried that nothing would come out, or that anything that did come out was not what she wanted to say.

'I don't ... I—' she broke off. She what? What *did* she want to say?

He moved closer until he was arm's length away from her. He touched one hand to her shoulder, then retracted it as if he'd been electrocuted. She could still feel the warmth of his fingers, even if his touch was brief.

'Alice,' she whispered. *Damn it*. She knew she'd say something she didn't want to know an answer to.

His jaw tensed, and his brow furrowed, but he didn't shut off. Not like he had previously. 'She would want me to be happy,' he said quietly. 'She'd want me to move on.'

'I wouldn't,' she blurted out, fully convinced the wiring between her brain and her mouth had been hijacked. The crease in his brow deepened. 'Want you to move on, I mean. I'd rather you … suffered.'

She felt her own brow crease as she processed what she'd said. God, he shouldn't catch her out like this. He should give some warning if he was going to confess everything. She'd never been good with being put on the spot.

'You'd want me to … suffer?' he repeated, his eyebrow shooting up in amusement.

She swallowed. 'I'm a selfish person,' she said. 'I get jealous. Not like, overbearingly jealous, but … jealous.' She felt like crawling into a shell and hiding for the foreseeable future. What was it about him that made her turn into a fool?

'For good reason,' he said, shrugging gently. 'Considering what you've been through.'

She felt her chest tighten. Was this how it would always be with them? That they'd always be bringing up their past relationships? Sure, hers was a complete failure, and, well, his followed the vows of *until death do us part* a bit too literally, but that didn't mean they had to bring it up all the time. But maybe that's how it would be—with him, with anything. Brett wasn't just some guy it didn't work out with. He was the father of her children. And that was something she couldn't change. She could never just forget about him. She could never not talk about him. She just had to grow used to that.

'I want you, Brooke,' he said, his tone deep, vibrating through her body in the way that made every one of her senses come alive. He lifted his hand to touch her cheek, then dropped it by his side before it touched. He let out a sigh. 'I want you as more than a friend. I want you to be the first person I message in the morning, the first thought in my mind, and the last. I want to call you mine, and I know that would make my life so much brighter.'

'Lewis,' she whispered, a traitorous tear rolling down her cheek.

'You don't have to say anything now,' he said, taking her hand in his. God, it felt so warm, so right. So terribly terrifying. 'Take as much time as you need. But I'll wait for you and the kids at the pool tomorrow morning. Come if there's even the slightest chance you'll give us a go, then take as long as you need for something more … definitive.'

Another tear rolled down her cheek, and he brushed it away with the backs of his fingers. His fingers left a hot trail across her cheek that sent her brain into more chaos than it already was. She closed her eyes, drooping her head, trying desperately to clutch onto any rational thought.

'I don't want to be your … rebound,' she whispered, surprising herself again with her choice of words. 'I can't compare with Alice,' she continued. 'I don't want to be the girl that got you back into the dating world, who was more convenient than anything. I'm not a rebound, Lewis.'

His hand cupped the back of her head and she felt his lips press softly against her forehead. Then, he let her go, and she felt that disappointment of losing his touch—incomplete, somehow. She opened her eyes to look into the striking blue-green of his, searching her with a warmth she couldn't comprehend.

'How could you be a rebound when you're the only one who made me realise I couldn't keep living in the past when the future could be so beautiful?'

His words hit her to her core, and she felt her breath catch again—something she was becoming all too familiar with. He smiled at her, sending her stomach flipping, even though she could tell he was still worried about what she would say. But he'd given her time. As long as she needed.

'If there's even the slightest chance,' he said, backing away slowly. 'If you come tomorrow, I'll know then.'

Then, he was gone, and she was on the verge of collapsing. She had as much time as she needed. She only had to decide if there was a chance—any chance at all. And she had a feeling she already knew her answer.

Chapter 12

'Maddie, come on! We've got to go!'

Maddie gasped, racing past her towards the door. 'Quick, Mum! We're going to be late!'

Brooke scoffed, still finding it amusing how Maddie could go from spending forty-five minutes eating a slice of toast to thinking she should be the one to round everyone up. '*Towel*,' she said, reminding Maddie for the twelfth time in the last half hour.

Maddie groaned, running back to the lounge room to grab the towel she'd dumped in there, then raced back to the door. 'Hurry, Mum! Gracie will be waiting for me!'

Brooke scooped up an excited Ollie in her arms and juggled the bags towards the door. Every time she left the house, she thought about how it would be so much easier to take the bags out first, *then* round the kids up. And every time, she still juggled everything out in one trip. After all, who had time for multiple trips from the house to the car when being late was already a regular occurrence?

She felt her stomach roll. Would he still be there? Would he wait for her, even though she was late? God, she'd tried so hard to be on time, too. She always did. Yet, somehow, she was always late whenever she had to go somewhere with the kids. Today was no exception, even when it was the one day she shouldn't be late. Not when it could determine her future.

She still had to think about what she wanted with him, but she knew there was a good chance she'd give him a go. Even if it was risking the kids getting hurt. That she would get hurt. And like he'd said, if there was even the *slightest* chance her answer would be yes, then she should go to the pool. If she didn't show up, he would take that as a no, and she might never hear from him again. God, she wasn't sure she could take that.

What would she do if he'd already left by the time she got there? She didn't know where he lived, where to find him. And she doubted he'd answer her calls or messages if she missed him.

'*Mum!*' Maddie whined, hanging on the door handle.

'I'm coming, I'm coming!' she said, hiking Ollie further up her hip and holding her pile of things in place with her chin. 'Open it up.'

Maddie fiddled with the lock and swung the door open, and Brooke almost tripped over her. Why did she stop? It wasn't until she heard a familiar voice speak that she realised why her daughter had frozen in place.

'Hi, Brooke.'

He was standing at the bottom of her porch steps, his hands in his pockets, looking almost exactly the same as he always did, though, perhaps, more mature. What was he doing here?

'Brett?'

***

She wasn't coming.

He'd thought she might have been running late, but she'd messaged him when she was running late for their previous playdate. Wouldn't she message him now? But this time was different. This time, he'd given her a choice he was starting to regret. He'd been so sure she would come. Wasn't there any chance at all?

He felt a wet hand tug on his and looked down at Gracie. 'Are they coming?' she said.

He sighed, taking another glance towards the gate. 'I don't think so, noodle,' he said.

*Damn it*. Why had he used the pool as his option? He hadn't thought of it when he said it. He hadn't thought of how it would affect Gracie, how it would make her sad if she didn't come. No, he should have used something where it would have only been him and Brooke, not the kids. But he'd been so sure, so certain she would have come—that there was a chance, even if it was slim. Obviously, she thought otherwise.

'Oh,' Gracie said solemnly, squeezing his hand tighter. 'Can we go, then?'

He nodded. 'Sure, honey,' he said. 'Go dry off.'

Clearly, it didn't matter what he thought. Everything he'd said meant nothing. He'd opened up, put his heart on the line. He'd told her what he wanted, and she obviously didn't reciprocate. So, there was no point in hanging around. After all, who was ever *that* late?

***

His lips quirked up into that crooked smile she'd once fallen for. He looked stronger than she remembered—he'd lost the belly he'd had since she knew him, and his shoulders were broader. He used to wear baggy clothes, now he was wearing those jeans that hugged his legs too tight for what she thought was really suitable for a man, and a shirt that was at least one size too small, more likely two.

He dropped his gaze to Maddie, who was still frozen in place, staring at him. 'Hey, Nug,' he said, stepping up onto the porch.

Brooke felt Maddie back up against her leg, then, the little girl ran back inside. Brooke heard what could only be the bedroom door slamming closed.

She lowered the bags to the floor, getting a better grip of Ollie, who'd also gone pretty still.

'What's her problem?' Brett said, nudging his head in the direction Maddie went, walking towards her.

'What do *you* think?' she said, fully intending for the sarcasm to be as obvious as it sounded.

He stopped walking, the smile dropping from his face. 'Brooke—'

'What do you want, Brett?'

He shrugged lazily. 'I wanted to see you,' he said. 'And the kids. Is this … him?'

'Ollie, yes, this is him,' she said, holding him a little tighter. 'Why the sudden change of heart?'

'Can't a guy see his kids when he wants to?'

'You haven't been back since you left,' Brooke said, leaning against the doorframe. 'You rarely call. You want to know why Maddie ran off? She's mad at you, Brett. You haven't visited, you haven't put in any effort to see her. Did you really think she'd be happy to see you? Heck, *I'm* mad at you.'

'I just want to be a part of their lives,' he said.

'Well, you should have thought of that when you left and didn't bother to keep a connection.'

'It's different now, Brooke,' he said, rubbing his forehead. 'I'm different. I can't … have … any more kids.'

'Wh—what?' He *what*? What did he mean by he couldn't have any more kids? He'd literally gotten her pregnant almost two years ago!

'Can I come in?' he asked, dropping his gaze to

the bags at her feet. 'Were you going out?'

'I was planning on it,' she mumbled.

'Can it wait?'

'I was meeting … someone,' she said, shifting Ollie's weight. He wasn't even squirming—surprisingly. Why did he still feel heavy when he stayed still?

'Please, Brooke?' he said, clasping his hands together. 'Can't you reschedule? Let me visit with the kids and we can talk it out.'

'I don't think rescheduling is an option,' she mumbled, moving to the side. After all, she was already so late she was worried Lewis wouldn't be there even if she did show up. 'Come in, Brett.'

But even as she said it, she couldn't help but feel her heart dropping to her stomach. She glanced at her car, aching to climb in and speed to the pool, praying to God he'd still be there. But he'd probably left already. And maybe he'd forgive her if she messaged him later. Maybe she'd call. God, Brett had the worst possible timing.

She closed the door and followed him into the lounge, placing Ollie on the floor with his toys. He eyed Brett suspiciously, pouting, clutching on to his favourite toy car. This kid had no idea who the man was sitting on the couch. *No* idea. He didn't know he was looking at his father. For all he knew, Brett was just some random off the street that was sitting in his house.

'Want a drink?' she said, folding her arms awkwardly across her chest. 'Tea, coffee? Beer? I think there might be one at the back of the fridge.'

'Coffee, please,' he said.

Her eyebrow lifted. 'Not drinking before lunch? You *are* different.'

'Like I said,' he said, his lips curving into the crooked smile. 'I've changed.'

She forced a smile onto her face, though she still wasn't entirely convinced, and went to the kitchen to make coffee. Ollie started crying almost as soon as she was out of sight, and she could hear Brett trying to soothe him, which only succeeded in making him scream louder. For some reason, it both tore at her and made her smile, and she didn't know why. Well, she knew why it tore at her—her kid had no idea who his father was, and his father had never bothered to hang around to even meet him or show any interest in him. But why did it make her smile? Maybe it was because it showed Brett he couldn't just walk back into their lives. Maybe because it would have annoyed her if Ollie took to him as soon as he saw him. Perhaps because Ollie didn't cry like that for Lewis.

*Lewis*.

She really screwed that one up, didn't she? She flicked her eyes to the clock on the wall and frowned, realising the time hadn't changed from when she'd last looked at it. *Shoot*. She tapped her pockets to look for her phone and came up empty—it must be in one of the bags she was going to take to the pool. That, or it was still near her bed. Ollie's screaming went to the next level, and she poured the milk into the coffees and carried them to the lounge room. Brett was standing up, jigging Ollie, looking worried.

'He was crying,' Brett said, his voice sounding stressed. 'I thought a cuddle would help, but he started crying louder.'

As soon as Ollie realised Brooke was back, he seemed to go dead weight on Brett, flopping his body towards her. She put the coffees on the coffee table and took him from Brett's arms. His crying turned into sobs that shook his little body, but at least he wasn't screaming anymore.

'He just doesn't know you,' she said.

Even *that* she wasn't entirely convinced on. He hadn't cried with Lewis, and he didn't know him either. Maybe it was the fact Lewis had a kid of his own and Brett was, well, bad with kids. Maybe Ollie could sense that. Could kids sense that kind of thing?

'I'm his father,' he said solemnly, sitting back on the couch, and taking his coffee.

'But he doesn't *know* you,' she repeated. 'Kids need time.'

'What about Maddie?'

'Time,' she said again. She attempted putting Ollie on the floor again, but he clung to her like a baby monkey. She pulled him close again and sat on the armchair. 'Hey, speaking of, you don't have the time, do you?' she added. 'The battery's flat in the clock out there and I'm not sure where my phone is.'

Brett nodded, the dazed look disappearing from his eyes, and checked his watch. 'Almost eleven thirty,' he said.

*Eleven-thirty*? God, she was a whole lot later than she thought. Here she was thinking she'd only been ten, fifteen minutes late, and she was an *hour and a half* late! She rested back against the armchair, her stomach twisting. She'd already missed her chance before she even realised. Surely, Lewis wouldn't have been waiting an hour and a half for her to show up. He would have given up well before that. Maybe everything was just working against her being with Lewis, especially with the damn clock dying on her, misplacing her phone, and her *ex* showing up wanting to be a part of the kids' lives. What the hell was going on? She'd almost wager her car wouldn't have started if she'd even managed to get out to it. It wouldn't surprise her one bit.

'Sorry, you missed your ... thing ... you were going to,' he said, bringing her back to reality.

'Playdate,' she offered. 'It was a playdate, but it seems I'd already missed it, so it's not really your fault. So,' she said, clearing her throat. She eased Ollie onto the floor now he'd stopped sobbing, and he returned back to staring at Brett while clutching his toy. She grabbed her coffee off the coffee table and took a sip. 'Why are things different now?'

'Straight into it, huh?' he smirked.

She stared at him. He shows up unannounced wanting to be more involved with the kids and he's surprised she jumped straight into it instead of engaging in small talk? She'd never been much of a small talk kind of person. She'd always been straight to the point. His smile dropped, and he shifted in his seat.

'Like I said, I can't have any more kids,' he said. 'I want to get to know Maddie and Ollie. I want them to know their father. I know I screwed up, but I can make it up to them. To you.'

She bit into her lip, unsure of what he was getting at. 'Why can't you have kids?' she prodded.

'I, umm,' he said, taking a deep breath. 'I had surgery—'

Her eyebrow lifted. 'You got a vasectomy?'

'—for prostate cancer.'

Her other eyebrow shot up and her mouth dropped. She hadn't seen that one coming. 'God, Brett,' she whispered. 'Why didn't you tell me?'

'I'm telling you now,' he said. 'I'm clear, but it made me see things differently, you know? It made me realise how much I screwed up.'

'I'm sorry you had to go through that,' she said. 'But it doesn't change things. You have a lot of making up to do—for Maddie, and Ollie. Not for me.'

He nodded. 'I get it,' he said. 'Does that mean you'll let me see them?'

She sighed. 'You've always been allowed to see them, Brett,' she said. 'It's on you. I'm sure Ollie will warm up to you, and Maddie—I'll talk to her, she might forgive you, but she might need time. It's not going to happen quickly, Brett, you need to realise that.'

'I do,' he said, genuinely looking appreciative. It was a look she was not used to seeing on him. 'Thank you.' He hesitated. 'And you?'

'What about me?'

'Will you forgive me?'

She took another sip and bit into her lip, mulling the question over. She didn't *hate* him. She might have when he first left, but she'd gotten over it. But forgiving him? Had she already done that? Or had it more been acceptance? She supposed, in a way, she'd forgiven him for leaving. But she was still mad at him for not keeping in touch with the kids.

'I'll forgive you,' she said, decidedly. 'When the kids forgive you.' He nodded, taking another gulp of his coffee that made *her* throat burn. She'd never understood how he could take big drinks of things that were still so hot. 'Do you have somewhere to stay?' she added. Last she'd heard, he'd moved away.

'I've got a motel room for now,' he said. 'Until I can find somewhere more … permanent.'

'You're moving back?' Why did it surprise her?

'The kids—I want to be near them. Having cancer made me realise I had to get my priorities right. I had to put you and the kids first.'

She squinted, feeling her body tense. She took a shaky breath. 'I'm nothing but the mother of your children, Brett.'

'You're much more than that, Brooke.'

'Not to you, I'm not,' she said, shaking her head.

He held her gaze for a moment too long, then polished off his coffee. Her cup was still burning her hands. 'We were in love,' he said, finally.

'*Were* being the keyword,' she mumbled. 'And

I'm not so sure, Brett. Being in love is a two-way street and usually doesn't involve cheating on the one you *love*.'

She thought she saw a muscle twitch along his jaw. He placed the cup on the coffee table. 'I thought you were over that,' he said coldly.

'Guess I'm not,' she said flatly. She perched herself on the edge of the seat. 'You should go, Brett.'

'Brooke—'

She put her hand up between them. 'You can see the kids,' she said. 'You can be a part of their lives. But nothing's going to happen with us. Understood?'

He nodded slowly, standing. 'If you're sure.'

'I am.'

'Will you—'

'I'll let you know,' she finished, rising to her own feet. 'When Maddie's ready. But I don't want to push her.'

He held her gaze for a moment. She'd once wondered, if she saw him again, would she still see the Brett she'd once fallen for? Or would she see the Brett that walked out that door? Would there be anything there, when she looked into his eyes? Would her feelings come crashing back as though he'd never left? But now, as she looked into those pale blue eyes, she knew her answer. He was a different Brett to either of the Brett's she knew. This one looked like he genuinely wanted to bond with his kids. He had changed, like he said. And when she checked her feelings, she felt ... nothing. She had no feelings for Brett. He was just the father of her children.

'Thank you, Brooke,' he said. Then, he was gone.

***

Lewis had almost made it home when he backtracked across town to go to her place. He was still in a state of disbelief, numbness. Why didn't she show? There was no message, no phone call. Nothing to explain why she bailed. Hadn't he read her right? What could have happened overnight to make her certain there was no chance at all?

He was a fool for giving her that choice. Why didn't he give her the time to process it? Why did he have to use their *playdate* as the discerning factor? Heck, he'd done nothing but disappoint Gracie—and that was the last thing he wanted to do. Well, he might be a fool, but he wasn't one to give up easily. And he wasn't going to give up on her. Not until it was clear she didn't want him. And if that meant going to her place and talking to her, and possibly beg a little, then so be it. At least then, he would have an answer.

'Daddy, where are we going?' Gracie said. She'd been quiet for the whole drive until now—totally out of her usual character.

'Just for a little drive, sweetheart,' he said.

'Why?'

'I've got to do something.'

'But we were almost home.'

'I know,' he said. 'I only just thought of it.'

'But I want to go home,' she mumbled.

He glanced into the rear-vision mirror and saw her saddened face. 'We will, soon,' he said. 'I just have to do this first.'

He didn't know what gave him the confidence to confront her. He'd felt so cool about the situation, like he had it under control. If she showed, he had a chance. If she didn't, he didn't. It was simple. Until she didn't show. His brain went wild with what he would say, but by the time he pulled up across the road from her place, he felt that confidence slip away quicker than it came.

He watched the blond-haired man walk down her porch steps with a smile on his face. He felt his stomach churn as the bastard adjusted his shirt and got in his car. He felt a lump settle in the base of his throat and his chest tighten as the son of a bitch drove off.

She hadn't been alone. And that … that … *grub* … sure as hell wasn't her brother.

'Why have we stopped, Dad?' Gracie said, bored, oblivious of what was going on in Lewis's head.

'No reason,' he mumbled, putting the car into drive again. 'Let's go home, shall we?'

'*Finally*,' Gracie groaned.

*Chapter 13*

Brooke pulled Maddie and Ollie into their nightly embrace on Maddie's bed. The same snuggle they had every night before she tucked them in. Maddie had been out of sorts all afternoon, and Brooke knew why. Seeing Brett shocked Maddie as much as it shocked her. And kids can be very fickle things. She just didn't know what to say to her. *Hey, your father's back, but we have no idea how long for?* She knew Maddie had the same fears she did. Could Brett really be true to his word? Changed man or not, he was still Brett.

'Honey, I think we should talk,' she started, stroking Maddie's hair as the little girl snuggled into her chest. 'About your dad.'

'Why was he here?' she mumbled.

Brooke pressed her lips to Maddie's forehead. 'He wanted to see you,' she said. 'And Ollie. Both of you.'

'I didn't want to see him,' Maddie said.

Brooke frowned, her heart aching for her girl. She'd thought Maddie had taken it hard when Brett left. She hadn't thought about how it might affect her when he came back. 'Why is that, honey?'

She felt Maddie shrug, then she pulled back when Ollie reached out to grab hold of her hair. Brooke pulled Ollie back, so he couldn't reach Maddie's hair. God, why did sitting still even have to be a problem?

'Because he left us,' Maddie said. She looked up at Brooke with those blue eyes that glistened like sun shimmering on the ocean. 'And he didn't want to come back.'

'But he's back now,' Brooke said. 'He wants to see you more.'

'But what if he leaves again?' A tear rolled down Maddie's cheek and Brooke wiped it away.

'It's just a risk we're going to have to take, sweetheart,' she said, kissing her again. 'Why don't we start small, huh? Maybe he could come over for dinner tomorrow. Would that be okay?'

Maddie thought for a moment, wrapping her arms tightly around her special bear. 'I think that would be okay.'

'Yeah? All right, then. We'll do that,' she said, sliding off Maddie's bed. She gave Ollie a kiss and placed him in his cot, then tucked them both in.

'Mummy?'

'Hmm?'

'What if he doesn't come?'

Brooke swallowed the lump in her throat. What *if* he didn't come? She would have negotiated on his behalf for nothing. 'He'll be there, darling. I promise.' Well, she hoped.

She left the door ajar behind her and went to the lounge room, flopping on the couch, taking in a deep breath. God, she hoped Brett was going to follow through with it. That he was going to be more involved with the kids' lives. If he didn't, he had no right to ever come back. She thought about his surgery and if it really had changed his perspective that much. Even if it had, what was to say he wouldn't go back to his old ways? At least, this time, there wouldn't be a them to think about. She just had to think about the kids. And she had to make sure they didn't get hurt—again.

She lifted her phone and hovered her thumb over the screen again. Over Lewis's name. He hadn't answered her calls all afternoon. Why should he now? She'd screwed up. God, she'd been running too late before Brett even showed up—she couldn't even blame him for it! She had to talk to him, had to tell him what happened. And hopefully, they could laugh about it. Though, she suspected that was a long shot. But she had to try. She took a shaky breath and hit the call button.

She was well aware she was holding her breath. And she had a feeling she would until he answered. *If* he ever answered.

***

Lewis grabbed a beer from the fridge and checked his vibrating phone. *Brooke*. Again. He ignored the call, went to the couch, and flicked the television on. He didn't really care what was on, as long as whatever he was watching could distract his thoughts from going *there*. He'd already put Gracie to bed, and it was the time between putting her to bed and him falling asleep that his thoughts often went wild. And it usually wouldn't bother him as much as he knew it would bother him today.

She didn't show.

He saw a man leaving her place.

Then, she spent all afternoon trying to call him. For what? To make up some excuse about why she couldn't go? Well, he suspected he already knew. There was no chance—none. She was already with someone else. And she hadn't told him. Or maybe that's why she was calling. To tell him what he already knew.

His phone buzzed again, and he checked it—a message. From Brooke. Like the sucker for punishment he was, he opened it up.

*Lewis, please call. We need to talk.*

He scoffed, taking a sip of his beer. Like *that* was going to get him to do anything. *We need to talk.* Wasn't that the throwaway line that preceded a dumping, saying it's not going to work? Not that it could really be a breakup, per se, since they weren't *actually* together. Even if their kiss had put an entirely different thought in his head.

*Their kiss.*

He understood why he kissed her—he found her irresistible, for starters, and he'd lost control of himself for a moment. But why did she kiss him back? Why did she pull them closer to the door, implying she wanted something more, if she was with some other guy? Or was that the kind of woman she was? Surely, not. She'd said her and Brett had ended because he'd cheated on her. That kind of thing does something to a person, and he didn't believe it would make her turn into a person that would cheat. So, what was going on? He took another sip of his beer and tapped out a message.

*Gracie's pretty upset you didn't show.*

He sent the message and focussed on the moving pictures on the television, though he didn't take any of it in. He knew it probably wasn't the *best* thing he could have said. But truth be told, he was pissed. At her, at himself, at everything to do with whatever it was they had. His phone buzzed again, and he looked at it.

*I'm sorry. I was on my way, but something came up.*

He frowned. If that wasn't the worst excuse he'd seen, he wasn't sure what would be.

*What came up?* he sent.

She tried calling again, and he ignored the call. Again. Shortly after, he got another message.

*Lewis, please?*

He took another sip of his beer as her name popped up on his screen again. He took a deep breath, and this time, he answered.

'What came up?' he said, well aware his voice sounded annoyed.

'I'm sorry, Lewis,' she said frantically, talking quickly. 'I was on my way, and I thought I wasn't running too late, but I couldn't find my phone to let you know. Then, something came up and I realised the clock I was going off had stopped and I was way later than I thought and I ... I—'

'*What* came up, Brooke?' he repeated.

'It doesn't matter,' she said softly. 'What matters is I was going to meet you, Lewis. And I was going with more than just a chance. I—I want to ... be ... with you.'

He felt his breath catch in his throat, and he wasn't entirely sure he could move his body if he wanted to. Earlier that day, he would have loved hearing her say that. In fact, he was sure nothing could have made him happier. But now? Now, it was like a bittersweet sting he couldn't shake.

'Lewis?' she said shakily.

He took a second to steady his breath and pinched the bridge of his nose with his thumb and forefinger. 'I'd hoped you would say that,' he said quietly. God, his voice sounded empty even to his own ears. 'When you came to the pool. But I don't know, Brooke. If you can't tell me what came up, then maybe I'm not as important to you as you are to me.'

He heard her sniff, and for a moment, he felt bad. But then he reminded himself he'd given her a choice. And he couldn't be with someone he couldn't trust and rely on.

'Lewis, y—you are important to me,' she sobbed. Damn it, now she was crying.

He fought the part of him that wanted to tell her it was okay, that they could try again. That could stop her from crying. But he knew it couldn't go that way. He knew from the start it could all go wrong, and they could all get hurt. And if tears were going to be shed, it was better now instead of down the track when things were a lot more serious.

'I saw him leave your place, Brooke,' he said flatly.

'What? Who?'

'Blond hair, cocky looking. So, if your *something* has something to do with him, then forget it. I don't want to be your second choice.'

There was silence on the other end and he wondered if it actually *was* what it had looked like. *Damn*. He wasn't even sure what to think now. Simply hearing her voice made him feel like an ass for thinking badly of her. But now? He generally knew silence as a confirmation, and in this instance, it did not feel good. He pulled the phone away from his ear enough to see the screen and readied himself to hang up. After all, what more was there to say? But her voice made him hesitate, and even though it wasn't against his ear, he still heard what she said.

'Brett showed up,' she said. 'Without warning.'

He pressed the phone to his ear again, leaning forward, his elbows on his knees. 'Your Brett?'

She sighed. 'The kids' father, yes,' she said. 'He's not … *my* Brett.'

'I thought he hasn't been in contact with you,' he said, rubbing his forehead.

'He hasn't,' she said. 'He showed up as I was walking out the door to meet you. He's the guy you saw leaving.'

He felt his jaw tense, feeling more of a fool for jumping to conclusions so quickly. 'What did he want?'

'He wants to be more involved with the kids,' she said. 'Or, so he says. I'm still not sure I believe him.'

'Has he given you reason to?'

'I don't know,' she said quietly. 'He seems to have changed. He's been through a lot since he left.'

'So have you.'

'He had cancer, Lewis,' she said slowly. 'If anything's likely to change someone, it's that. I just … hope … he's as genuine as he's making out to be.'

'So, you've agreed to let him see the kids?'

'Of course, I have.'

'And you?'

'What about me?'

'Is he trying to get back together with you?' Even the thought of it made his chest ache. How could he go from being pissed to being a jealous boyfriend so quickly?

'I already told him nothing is going to happen,' she said, hesitantly.

'But it *is* what he was wanting to do?'

She hesitated a moment. 'I don't know,' she said. 'And I don't care, because I want you, Lewis. Do you believe me?'

He squeezed his eyes shut, knowing, in his heart, what his answer would be.

***

She was still in a bit of disbelief at the fact he even bothered replying to her message, let alone finally answering her call and hearing her out. So, he'd seen Brett. That would explain why he'd been avoiding her then. She'd thought it was just because she didn't show up.

She realised she was holding her breath for most of their conversation and waiting for his response was no exception. She swiped at the tears rolling down her cheek. She hadn't even thought about what she might say if he said he didn't believe her. She'd been honest with him—she *did* want to be with him, she *was* on her way to see him. She *had* honestly thought she wasn't running as late as she was. And she wished Brett hadn't shown up on her doorstep. But he had. And there was nothing she could do about it now.

What could she do? She couldn't deny him seeing her kids and risk him taking her to court trying to get custody of them after she'd spent all this time being the *only* parent to them. Would he do that? Maybe not. But, since he's a *changed man,* she didn't know what he would or wouldn't do. She didn't want to risk it. And she wouldn't like to put her kids through that. After all, she didn't have a problem with Maddie and Ollie seeing Brett—he was their father. And he would probably make a good father if he tried. But how would *that* affect what she could have with Lewis?

'I believe you,' he said, finally, snapping her out of her thoughts. He believed her? So, he was giving her another chance? 'But,' he added slowly. He wasn't? She should have figured that would be coming. 'I don't think we should rush things.'

'So, wh—what are you saying?' She tried not to get her hopes up, in case that was his way of saying it wasn't going to happen.

'I'm saying we should go slow,' he said, decisively. 'Give you time to process Brett being back, hang out with the kids a bit, and maybe … try that going out thing again. You and me.'

She felt her heart skip a beat, and she was sure something was trying to squirm out of her stomach. All afternoon, she'd been so worried she'd blown it, blown her only chance with him. Yet, here he was, telling her he wanted to try things with her. Take it slow—he wanted to take it slow. What did that even mean? Did that mean what she *tried* to do at the end of their date was entirely off-limits? Or did it just mean he was serious about her? God, she hoped it was the latter. After all, she was getting *very* serious about him.

'I'd like that,' she said, breathlessly, despite her

efforts to steady her breathing.

'Good,' he said, clearing his throat. If she imagined what he was doing, she could see him reclining back—on the couch maybe, or his bed. 'So, Miss Cottle, what are your plans for the night?'

'I'm just relaxing on the couch at the moment,' she said, sighing, closing her eyes and imagining him next to her. Imagining his leg brushing against hers, his arm around her shoulder. His lips pressing against his hair. 'Just … umm … thinking about making a cup of tea. I might get to enjoy it hot.' She heard him laugh, a deep, rich sound that seemed to vibrate through her body. It was almost as though he was here. 'What about you?' she added, smiling.

'I've got a beer,' he said. 'I was going to watch some tele, but I have … no … idea … what on earth is playing at the moment. Besides, my plans have changed.'

'How so?'

She was aware her smile probably looked goofy, and she felt like a teenage girl with a school-girl crush. For just a moment, she didn't feel like a single busy mother of two. She felt like there was only her and the handsome guy on the other end of the line.

'Well, my dear,' he said, the sound of his voice shifting as though he was standing up and moving. 'I just got a call from a beautiful woman, and I have a feeling I might be talking to her for a while.'

She felt her cheeks flush, and her whole body heated up a degree. Or ten. 'Oh really?' she said. 'And are you okay with that?'

'Damn right, I am,' he chuckled. She heard what sounded like a bottle clattering in a tub, then a moment later, she heard the soft thud of a door closing. Then, his voice grew deeper, sexier, and her body almost quivered with the shock. 'Are you?'

'Mhmm,' she hummed, her voice hitting a pitch much higher than she intended.

'Do you have your tea?' God, she could listen to that voice all day. Rich, velvety, rolling through her with an intensity she didn't know a phone call could make her feel.

'N-no,' she stammered.

'Are you going to have one?'

'I—I'm not … sure,' she said, squinting. Why did putting words together in a coherent sentence seem especially hard tonight?

He chuckled again, and it just about sent her stomach flipping. She sunk further into the couch, wishing more and more—hoping—that the whole taking it slow thing didn't mean having a whole lot of off-limits.

'Brooke?' he said, his voice sounding almost *too* good coming from his mouth.

'Hmm?' she hummed, spreading her hand across her stomach to make sure it was staying put. The sensations of her fingertips running across it made her realise it seemed a whole lot more sensitive than usual. God, this guy was going to ruin her before she even saw him again.

'Can I ask you something?'

She nodded, then realised he couldn't see her.

She slowly opened her eyes and sat up straighter, realising she was too close to falling asleep. Though, his voice was so soothing, how could she *not* feel relaxed with him talking? 'Sure,' she said.

There was a pause at the other end—just for a moment—then he spoke. If she'd thought his voice before was deep and sexy, then she had her standards low, because now, it reached a whole other level of sexy. 'The other night, on our date,' he said slowly. She hummed, waiting for him to continue. 'What … umm … what colour were your panties?'

She covered her mouth, feeling the intense smile beneath her hand. Had her stupid rambling made him keep thinking about that all night and since then? God, no wonder he'd acted strangely at certain moments that night. 'Blue,' she whispered. 'Lace, if that helps.' New ones, at that. Specifically bought for that date. But perhaps she'd leave that part out.

She heard a groan from the other end and it made her smile widen even more—if that was possible. 'Light or dark?'

She hummed. 'Dark.'

'And now?'

God, her smile was starting to make her cheeks ache. She bit into her lip, shifting her tone to be as seductive as she could manage. Were they really doing this? Were they really going into the sexy talking on the telephone? Well, perhaps there was hope for their taking it slow, after all.

'What if,' she said, making her voice sound

breathy. 'What *if* I'm not wearing any?' There was silence again at the other end, and she wondered if she'd crossed a line. 'Lewis?' she said hesitantly.

He cleared his throat. 'A-are you?'

She eyed down her body, her oversized bedtime shirt coming half-way up her thighs. Oh, she was wearing some all right. Old, comfortable, trusty grey ones. Definitely not appealing to look at, and quite the opposite of what inspired any kind of sexy talk.

'I don't have to be.'

# Chapter 14

'Thanks again, Mum,' Lewis said, watching as Gracie ran into Gladys's arms.

This time, he'd decided *not* to give any details to Gracie—especially after how she blurted it all out to Gerald and Eve. Sure, it worked out for the better in the end on *that* particular instance. But he knew Gladys couldn't know about Brooke. Not yet. And as far as he knew, Brooke's parents didn't know either. He figured they'd have to tell them sometime soon, but for now, he wanted Brooke to himself. Then again, he knew they could only keep it a secret for so long. Especially since their parents were the ones looking after their kids.

'Mhmm,' Gladys mumbled, giving Gracie a kiss. Gracie raced off to put her bag in her room, and

Lewis knew he had about twenty seconds to give his mother enough information to keep her satiated, but not enough to actually give anything away. 'What did you say you were going to do with your free time?'

'I didn't,' he said, giving her a quick kiss on her cheek. 'I'm having some drinks with some friends. You know, a *proper* birthday celebration.'

It wasn't *entirely* a lie. Sure, he knew Gladys would think he meant with Drew and Miles, even though he didn't specify who he'd be with. And it would only be with one other person, instead of more. But if things went well, it could very well be considered a proper birthday celebration. Even if it was a few weeks late.

'What time will you pick her up?'

'Sometime tomorrow,' he said. 'Do you have anywhere you need to be?'

'I suppose not,' she mumbled. 'Just don't get too drunk, okay?'

'You worry too much, Mother,' he said, registering Gracie hopping back into the room. 'I won't,' he added. 'I'll just be too late to pick Gracie up tonight.'

'Where are you going, Daddy?' Gracie said, flinging her arms around him, and looking up at him with her big brown eyes.

He tugged one of her curls and watched it bounce back up into place. 'You don't need to worry your pretty little head over what I'm doing, noodle,' he said, smiling. 'I hear Nanna has a whole evening of fun planned with you.'

Gracie's eyes widened, and she bounced excitedly, glancing over at her Nanna. 'Really? Are we watching movies and eating popcorn and having a party?'

Gladys's eyebrow lifted, and she shot a look towards Lewis. He couldn't help but find it amusing. 'I think your father has overestimated what I have planned,' she said. 'But don't worry, sweetheart, we'll think of something to do.'

He smiled, bending down to give Gracie a kiss and started backing towards the door. 'Well, you two have fun,' he said, trying not to sound too excited. 'I've got to go.'

He registered the look on Gladys's face as he closed the door behind him. Yes, it was only a matter of time before she forced the truth out of him. Hopefully, by then, he would have enjoyed having Brooke to himself. All to himself.

***

It was smaller than she imagined it would be. For some reason—she supposed because of how big Gladys's house was—she'd thought Lewis's would have been bigger. But it was just a normal house, a little on the small side, even. Though, not as small as hers. It was, however, modern, a newish building— three, four years old, maybe. And as she looked at it, she could tell it suited him. Heck, she wouldn't mind living in a place like that, if she could afford it.

Nervously, she walked up to the door and tapped

on it. They hadn't seen each other since they'd sort-of-officially got together. But they had talked on the phone, and *those* conversations had gone well. Really well. She felt her cheeks flush at the memory of the first one of those conversations and every one that followed. She startled as she heard the lock click on the door and instinctively shot her hands up to cover her cheeks.

'Hey,' Lewis said, his smile wide and making her stomach flip. He looked genuinely happy to see her, and it sent her stomach twisting in a way she knew she could get used to feeling every time she saw him. His brow furrowed, but his lips were still lifted. 'You okay?'

'Mhmm,' she hummed, her pitch noticeably higher. She dropped her hands to smooth out her dress—okay, she *might* have put a bit of effort into dressing up for him. Or a lot. 'Why do you ask?'

'You look flushed,' he said, stepping to the side. She walked through the doorway, hoping she didn't look as shaky as she felt. God, she could swear her knees might give way at any moment.

'Really?' she said, feigning ignorance. She was all too aware her cheeks were burning. 'It is a bit hot outside,' she continued awkwardly, hoping it *was* actually hot—she hadn't been able to tell the difference in temperature all afternoon.

She stopped walking as soon as she'd passed him, realising it was going to be that awkward first-time-visiting thing of following him around through the house. She registered the door clicking behind her and scanned the part of the house she could see. Closed door on the right that she assumed was the master bedroom, another closed door slightly further up on the left that must be the garage. Straight ahead would be the kitchen, dining, and living area as most houses with open-plan living had now. Realising it might be a squeeze to let him pass her, she angled herself sideways to look back at him, startling again as his hand found its way around her waist to the small of her back.

His lips were on hers, and it took her a second to relax into it. Mostly because she was surprised to start with, and because she hadn't expected it. Not yet. Even if he'd said on the phone he wanted to kiss her the second he saw her again. She felt her knees grow weaker at the thought of what *else* he would follow through with. His lips moved against hers, gently, deliberately, and she could feel the last logical train of thought slip from her mind. Her lips cooperated fully without hesitation, and she felt his body press against hers. God, could they just skip the dinner and go straight to the end? They didn't have far to go until that closed door on the right could be swung open, and right now, she would be totally okay with that. His right hand traced her jawline, then cupped the side of her neck, his thumb stroking her cheek as he broke the kiss, pulling back enough to look her in the eyes.

She heard a moan, and judging by the smile on his face, she realised it came from her. She felt the heat race to her cheeks again and held onto his arms as gently as she could manage in an attempt to keep her legs from giving out beneath her. He lifted his hand from her lower back and tucked her hair behind her ear—she'd left it out tonight and was starting to regret it since she felt like she was a thousand degrees. But that might have had something to do with the tingling his fingers left everywhere they touched, and the kiss that might have actually been a whole lot more innocent than she'd realised. God, it had been too long.

'Hello, beautiful,' he whispered, his eyes dancing and his touch still sending sparks shooting to her core.

'Hey, stud,' she said, trying to find any coherent thought. His eyebrow lifted, his lips curved up in an amused smile. 'Handsome,' she corrected. 'Hello … handsome. You're a very handsome stud, did you know that? Man. A very … sexy … man.'

*Oh, God.* She was worse at this than she'd thought. Then again, she didn't exactly have experience in the complimenting a guy department. It wasn't the kind of talk that happened between her and Brett. The relationship they'd had could probably be more closely defined as friends with benefits, then with complications. She'd never felt weak in the knees like Lewis made her feel, never felt like she could lose control of her body at any moment. Never felt like she had to rely on someone else to keep her upright. And all Lewis had to do was smile at her.

He swept another quick kiss across her lips that had her insides squirming, wanting more, and linked his fingers with hers, leading her down the hallway. 'Do you like lamb shanks?' he said.

'Hmm? Y-yes,' she stammered, still trying to sort her thoughts out. 'How have you done them?'

She felt the pang of disappointment when he released her hand, reaching for a wine glass and filling it halfway. 'Slowly,' he said, indicating with his head to the casserole dish sitting on the stove, covered in foil. 'Wine?'

She nodded, taking the glass from his hand. He turned to the casserole dish. 'I thought you only knew how to make spaghetti,' she teased as he peeked under the foil.

'Why's that?'

'Your story,' she said, sipping her wine, grateful for the liquid courage it offered. 'Where Gracie got her nickname from. I just assumed—'

'That I couldn't cook,' he finished, glancing up at her. Though, he didn't seem offended. 'I can see how you came to that,' he continued, grabbing a bowl of mashed potato, and divvying a serving up on two plates. 'I've always been able to cook—one of my hidden skills, I suppose. It's just that spaghetti was the only thing Gracie would actually eat for a while.'

'That makes sense, then,' she mumbled, taking another big sip of her wine. She was sure that, pretty soon, she wouldn't be able to tell if she could barely keep herself upright because of Lewis or the wine.

He busied himself with serving the lamb shanks on the mashed potato. 'Make yourself at home,' he said.

She nodded, scanning the room around them. He had more things than she imagined a single guy might have. His house was well-furnished but neat. She saw some picture frames on the display table along the wall and absent-mindedly walked over to look at them. There seemed to be quite a few pictures of Lewis and Gracie, some even with Gladys in them. They made her smile. She sipped her wine some more as her eyes drifted to another picture. She picked it up.

It was unmistakably Lewis in the picture. But he was with someone else—a woman. Brown, curly hair, round brown eyes, slightly tanned skin. She looked like a grown-up version of Gracie. She was pretty, and they looked happy. Lewis looked happy. He looked in love. Brooke couldn't help but feel her heart sink to her stomach. She knew she shouldn't be jealous of this woman—Gracie's mother, she safely presumed. God, Lewis had to deal with Brett being back in town, but at least he knew it ended between her and Brett because it wasn't right. How could she compete with someone who died?

She felt her eyes burning, and she wasn't sure if she could stem it down to being tipsy—which was quite possible, since she'd barely eaten all day and had just about finished this glass of wine—or straight-up jealous of a dead person. Both made her look pathetic. She heard Lewis set the plates on the table and quickly blinked back the unshed tears. She could feel him standing just behind her, felt his arms wrap around her waist from behind, his cheek resting

against her head. God, it felt so good, but so …
confusing. Would he ever be able to love her like he
loved Alice? Great, now she was thinking about love.

'Is this … her?' she said, her voice cracking
slightly. Stupid voice.

'Alice, yes,' he said, sighing, squeezing his arms a
little tighter around her waist. 'It is.'

'She looks like …'

'Gracie?'

'Gracie,' she whispered. 'So much.'

'I know,' he said. He squeezed her again and
released her. She wished he hadn't. She didn't want
to miss his touch as much as she did. Especially when
he was still right there. It didn't make sense to her,
but it's how she felt. 'I … umm … I actually forgot
about that picture,' he said. 'It was Gracie's idea to
put it there. I can put it away if you like.'

'No,' she said, almost too abruptly. 'No, please
don't. I'm just being silly. Keep it there, for Gracie.'

She placed the picture back where it was and
turned to face him. He didn't look convinced. Heck,
*she* wasn't even convinced. She was sure she'd be
able to see pictures of Gracie's mother without
feeling jealous, eventually. But she wasn't sure how
long that would be. Maybe when she'd earned her
place amongst the pictures.

'You sure?' he said, rubbing his hands up and
down her arms. 'I can put it away if it makes you
uneasy.'

'No, not  uneasy,' she said, sighing, her shoulders
drooping with his touch. She squeezed her eyes shut.

'I don't know. I just got a little … jealous … that's all. But I'm okay, really.'

She felt his hand leave her left arm and nudge her chin up, she opened her eyes. This was their first *actual* date and she was already a crazy jealous girlfriend. But when she looked in his eyes, they weren't annoyed, or frustrated. But rather, amused. She pouted.

'Darling, *you* have nothing to be worried about,' he said softly. He pressed his lips to her right cheek. 'There's no competition.' He kissed her left cheek. 'I only want *you*.' He rested his lips again on her forehead and pulled back enough to look her in the eyes again. 'Understood?'

She nodded, continuing to pout until he pressed his lips to hers in a soft, chaste kiss. Not rushed. Just them. Like they had all the time in the world. Until her stupid stomach growled. She felt his lips curve into a smile against hers, and he broke away.

'Shall we eat?'

***

She'd been jealous of Alice. He didn't know why that made him smile. She didn't come across as the crazy jealous type, but he did think it was cute. God, at least *she* didn't have to see Alice, ever, except in pictures. He couldn't say the same for himself. He had to see Brett. Especially now he'd decided he wanted to be a part of the kids' lives. He'd never thought he was the jealous type, but there was something about knowing his girlfriend's ex was going to be spending time with her and the kids—possibly even taking time out of *him* getting to spend time with them—that he was finding particularly frustrating. *Girlfriend*. He hadn't labelled it before now, but that's what Brooke was, right? What else could she be?

The girl he had phone calls with that were definitely *not* safe for work, who he kissed when he saw her, who he cooked for. The girl who *dressed up* for a home date with him. The girl he couldn't keep his hands off and somehow managed to make him feel whole again, where even her smile made him want to take her, have her. The girl he snuck cuddles and kisses to as they cleaned up the dishes together. The girl he'd made promise to wear those blue lace panties, so he might get a chance of seeing them this time. The beautiful, sexy woman who felt more than right snuggled into his side as they watched the television together. Some ... weird ... movie that made absolutely no sense, especially since he was only thinking about one thing.

Brooke.

And how he wanted more of her.

So much more of her that it was driving him crazy trying to do something other than kiss her, touch her, have her. He slid his fingers up her arm, tracing lazy circles on her soft skin. He kissed the top of her head, breathing her in—the sweetness of her shampoo and perfume, her. God, it was the kind of thing he knew would make him addicted to her.

Heck, he already was.

'What was this movie about?' she mumbled.

'I have no idea,' he said, kissing her head again. He felt her body heave as she took a deep breath in.

'Your mum got Gracie for the night?' she said, almost … nervously.

'Mhmm,' he hummed, squeezing her shoulder softly. 'I think she suspects something's up.'

'Mmm,' she said, wiggling her shoulders, slipping a little closer to him. 'Mine do, too.'

His body was burning where hers rested against him. Heck, the movie probably *was* interesting, it was just impossible to think about anything else with this sexy woman next to him. His hand slipped off her arm as she wriggled a little closer again, falling onto her hip. She'd pulled her legs up on the couch earlier on, tucking them up beside her. Her shoes barely made it through dinner. He started tracing the lazy circles on her hip, until his hand rested lower, naturally, on her ass. He could feel her breaths growing shallow, quicker, and he could see her eyes wide, focussing on the television, though he suspected her mind was elsewhere. Probably with his.

'Have they got the kids?' he asked, squeezing his hand. She took in a sharp breath, and it made his lips curve higher. God, he wanted her.

'Georgie's looking after them,' she said, almost breathlessly. 'At my place, so Mum doesn't get too suspicious.'

He squeezed again and felt her press back against

his hand. He felt a rumble at the base of his throat, and he knew she was going to be the death of him. 'She expecting you home tonight?'

In the dim light of the lamp and the television, he could see the smile creep onto her face, hesitantly, as if she was trying to hide it. Her feet slipped off the couch, and she shifted enough to look him in the eyes. God, she was beautiful. And her eyes said everything he needed to know.

'No,' she whispered. 'She is not.'

His eyebrow lifted, his body feeling more alive than it had ever felt before. 'Is that so?' It sounded more like a growl than anything, but he didn't care. His need for her was primal, instinct. A pure necessity that he needed to live.

She bit into her lip, straightening up, sneaking her hand up, over his shoulder, until her fingertips traced a slow, sexy line up and down the length of his neck. 'Mhmm,' she hummed.

That's all he needed. His mouth was on hers, kissing her with an intensity, a passion she matched. He pulled her closer, one hand on her ass, the other cupping the back of her head as he searched her, swiping a pattern in her mouth, her tongue dancing with his. She was sweet, the taste of wine and lamb lingering, mixed with something totally and uniquely her that he couldn't resist. He could never resist her, now he'd had a taste. Not that he would ever want to.

She wrapped both arms around his neck, intensifying the kiss, and tucked her legs up under her—kneeling, almost, but resting on her legs. She wanted this. She wanted it as much as he did. And he was not in the mindset of disappointing. What the lady wants, she shall have. *That* is the mindset he's in. He slid his hands down her thighs, down to her knees, then back up again—this time, under her dress. Her dress that suddenly seemed like too much material to have on her. He hiked his hands back up her side, over her lace panties, and slid his hands to the small of her back, pressing her closer, pressing his own body against hers.

Her hands slid down his neck, across to his chest, and began to fiddle with the buttons of his shirt. He kissed her harder as she fiddled and moved to kiss her neck as she broke away to focus on the buttons. The damn buttons! The blasted things were fiddly enough without being under pressure. He felt the first one come undone, and her hands slid to the next one. But he was quickly running out of patience. He stopped her hands with his and yanked on his shirt, the buttons popping off. He might have ruined his shirt, but hey, at least that dealt with the blasted buttons.

'Lewis!' Brooke shrieked, laughing. 'You wrecked your shirt!'

He moved his hand up to cup her cheek, smiling, leaving kisses along her jawline and up to her mouth. 'I've got another,' he said, shrugging.

Her hands ran over his chest, up to his shoulders, brushing his shirt off. 'But I liked this one,' she mumbled against his lips, pressing herself against his bare chest.

He broke the kiss, pouting, resting his forehead against hers. 'I'm sorry, sweetheart, but I couldn't wait any longer.'

She shimmied back a little, matching his pout. 'Wait for what, exactly?' she said, wriggling her shoulders enough for one strap to shimmy off her shoulder and give him a better view of her cleavage.

He felt his lips curve into a mischievous smile, his eyebrow lifting. He shrugged his arms out of his shirt, leaving it on the couch. 'Want me to show you?'

She bit into her lip again, dropping her shoulder— and her strap—a little more, tilting her head to the side and looking up at him through her thick eyelashes. 'Mhmm.'

He slid off the couch, swooping her up in his arms, and carried her—shrieking—to his bedroom, and dropped her on his bed. She laughed, a rich sound that filled him, fuelling him with desire and making it harder for him to take his time.

'Oh, Mr Rieder,' she said dramatically, shimmying up the bed. 'Ride … me?'

Her brow furrowed as though she'd just realised what she said, and his eyebrow shot up again. Her cheeks darkened, but she had no reason to be embarrassed, in his opinion. He slid his belt off but kept his pants on, so he'd have *some* amount of control.

'Oh, honey, I fully intend to,' he said, smirking.

She pouted again, batting her eyelids. 'But not yet?' she said disappointedly.

He took his watch off, dropping it on the floor at the end of his bed where he expected her dress would end up, and knelt on the bed. 'I promised we'd take it slow,' he said, well aware his voice was uncontrollably deeper than usual. He crawled slowly up the bed towards her.

She bit into her lip. 'And by slow, you mean ...'

He settled himself above her, his legs nestled between hers, his lips hovering over hers. '*Slow.*'

He heard her moan as his lips met hers again, and he kept true to his word. He kissed her slowly, deeply, knowing they had the time, that they wouldn't be interrupted, and wanting her to enjoy every *slow* second of it. His fingertips traced up and down her thigh *slowly*, reaching a little higher each time. When he'd almost reached as high as he could go, he swapped to his other hand and did the same on that side. He kissed and caressed her until she was squirming, aching for more of his touch. Then, he gave her more.

He moved his lips south, over her chin, down her neck, across her collarbone in both directions, leaving a trail of kisses until her breathing was hot and heavy, her back arcing, pressing her chest closer to him as he kissed the mounds of her breasts—the parts that showed above her dress—her body begging him to give her more. So, he did.

Slowly, he slid down her body, breathing through the thin fabric of her dress, his hands shimmying it up her body as her fingertips dug into his shoulders until he reached the blue lace that stood between them. He pressed his mouth to her and heard her breath suck in as his hot breath dampened the lace. She squirmed again, pressing her heels against his back. He could have her now. God, he wanted to. But he'd promised slow. His hands continued shimmying her dress higher, his lips trailing up her stomach, kissing, sucking as they went. After an agonisingly slow journey, his hands reached for her breasts and he looked up, shocked. Something wasn't there that should be. Her eyebrow lifted, and her bottom lip was growing pale where she still bit into it.

***

Her heart was just about pounding out of her chest, and she was certain she'd either stopped breathing or was breathing so fast it seemed like she wasn't breathing at all. He was torturing her, he had to be. There was no other way to describe it. He was pushing her to the edge, to the brink, and not letting her go beyond. He was taking it *slow*. Screw slow! Well, that's exactly what she wanted to do. Slow, and fast. She wanted it all. She wanted *him*. And his attention was the most beautiful thing she'd ever felt, and possibly the most agonising.

But his look was priceless.

He flipped the dress up over her breasts, and her smile widened. 'Sweetheart,' he said, slowly.

'Hmm?' she hummed, pressing her body against him. God, why wouldn't he just give it to her?

'Wh—where's your bra?' he said, his eyes resting

on the mounds between them.

She'd always been worried she was going to get those post-baby boobs. And though Ollie had never taken well to breastfeeding, she'd been convinced she wouldn't have her old boobs back. Then again, they had returned to *almost* the size they were before babies. Even if they weren't quite as perky as they were before, she was still proud of them. She shrugged lazily, her smile widening, pressing her body against his again.

'Who needs one?' she said as seductively as she could.

She took in another sharp breath as he rolled her peaks between his thumbs and forefingers. God, he *was* torturing her. His eyes were flashing, wicked, almost. He knew what he was doing to her, and the bastard wasn't going to stop until she was begging. Well, she wouldn't pass it off as something she wouldn't do under this kind of duress.

'You just keep surprising me, don't you, Brooke?' he said, his voice deep—a rumble almost—vibrating through her body and pushing her even closer to the edge.

His mouth replaced one of his hands and he sucked and teased until she was unintentionally squirming again. Then, he swapped, giving her other breast the same amount of attention as the first. She reached for the button on his pants, but he was just out of her reach. *Damn it*! She moaned again— another thing she hadn't thought would be something she'd do. Then again, anything seemed possible right now.

He chuckled, glancing up at her, sliding her dress higher until it was over her head and *finally* off. 'Patience, love,' he teased. 'You need to be patient.'

'I *can't*,' she whined, pouting again. He met her lips with his again, and leaned on one arm, his body resting against hers, his free hand tracing patterns down her side, across her stomach, down her thigh, back up again.

'Yes, you can,' he said, breaking the kiss, studying her eyes.

'N—no, Lewis,' she said, breathlessly. 'I really can—oh!'

His fingers—his very dangerous, very naughty fingers—had flicked her lace panties to the side and had found their way home. His lips curved into a wicked smile at his discovery and she wasn't sure if she wanted to slap him for torturing her or start begging him shamelessly to take her now. He'd given her a whole new appreciation for the concept of *caress*, that was for sure. She pressed against his hand.

'Eager, are you?' he teased, sliding his hand rhythmically. Torturously.

'*Lewis*,' she pleaded, clutching his shoulders.

He laughed again, and she threw her head back against the pillows. God, if this was how she was going to die, she couldn't have planned it better. 'What?' he said. 'What do you want, Brooke? Say it.'

'You! I want you, damn it!' she shrieked, she reached down and grasped onto his wrist. '*Please*.'

'Well, if the lady insists,' he said, reaching for the drawer of the bedside table.

'I do, I *do* insist,' she pleaded.

He rolled off her, his dangerous hand going with him. In a few moments that certainly weren't *slow*, he'd had his pants off—her panties joining them at the end of the bed—and he'd poised himself above her, touching her—just—where he needed to go.

'You didn't need help?' she teased.

'Oh, honey, I was ready when you got here.' He nestled closer, resting, but still not there. 'Are you sure you want it?'

She groaned, lifting her hips, and his lips closed on hers, kissing her with a ferocity that awakened every sense in her body, and he drove home, right where he belonged, right where she was ready to beg him to go the second she walked through his door. And the very thought of *lovemaking* made so much more sense than it ever had before. He was perfect. *This* was perfect. And she knew she'd never again be able to imagine anything even close to that with anyone other than him.

God, she was screwed.

Chapter 15

Brooke paced the lounge room again, bouncing and shushing the little boy in her arms. She'd tried everything she could think of—nappy change, a bottle he refused, pain medication that ended up with almost more on his shirt than she was sure ended up in his mouth. Heck, she'd even attempted stripping him down for a bath and *that* didn't work. She'd tried a wet washer on his face, singing to him, trying to distract him with toys and books, bringing him into bed with her. *Nothing* was helping. Nothing was stopping him from crying. He didn't have a fever, or a rash, or anything physical she could put it down to.

She just assumed it was teething, growing pains maybe. She'd heard of a sleep regression around his age, but did it count if he'd never slept well? She was running on empty, just about in tears herself—heck, she was *sure* she'd already been crying. She'd sent Maddie back to bed when his crying had woken her, but now she was desperate for another adult to be there. Someone to help her out, to even just *hold* Ollie for just a few minutes so she could try to regain her sanity for a very, very brief moment.

She was tired. Exhausted. And she was sure she could sleep for days if she was given the chance. But she'd needed sleep since before Ollie was born. Even while she was pregnant with him, he'd affected her sleep. God, it was different to when Maddie was this age. She was only realising now how good she'd had it with Maddie. Sure, there'd been things that frustrated her, but at least she'd always been a good sleeper. Ollie was the opposite in every way, and nothing that ever helped with Maddie seemed to help with him.

She wanted to feel like she did with Lewis—like she finally had some time to herself. Almost two weeks had passed since that night, and since then, they'd done little more than stolen a quick kiss when the kids weren't watching. The only time they got any further was on their phone calls. They both still had work with only landing one full day off together. They both still had things to do that meant they couldn't just drop everything. They had kids. And kids—especially hers, it seemed—required a lot of attention.

It was almost as though, since they'd decided to

really give them a go, it was growing harder and harder to organise a way to spend as much time together as possible. And she missed him everywhere in between, even though she'd never missed anyone *that* much before. But Lewis made her feel differently than she had with anyone else. Simply seeing his smile had her questioning everything she thought she knew about relationships. About love. Wasn't love something you learned to do? That developed with time? Maybe it was her sleep-deprived, frustrated, and almost-breaking-from-the-crying brain talking, but she was sure there wasn't really anything else to call it. She was falling for Lewis, and she was falling hard.

Ollie kicked it up a notch, his crying growing more and more desperate as she rocked him side to side. She couldn't think about Lewis right now. She couldn't think about love and whether or not that's what she felt. She just had to make it through the night. Make it through tomorrow after she'd had a sleepless night. Just what she needed on her day off, right? To be recovering from a horrible night.

She searched for her phone, shifting Ollie's weight to one side when she found it, and scrolled through the numbers. She needed help. And she knew exactly who to call. Why should it matter it was the middle of the night?

'Brooke?'

Her heart skipped a beat when she heard his sleepy voice. Should she be doing this? Should she be calling him in the middle of the night, relying on him to help her when the kids gave her grief? But that's what he wanted, right?

'Brooke, is everything all right?'

She swallowed the lump in her throat, still jigging a howling Ollie on her hip. It's what she had to do, so why did she feel so apprehensive about it, like she was making the wrong choice?

'Now's your chance,' she said.

'What?'

She sighed, sure her voice sounded somewhere between annoyed and on the verge of crying. 'If you want to be more involved with the kids, now's your chance.'

***

'Morning, sweetheart,' Lewis said, stretching.

Gracie grunted, climbing into his bed, and snuggling up next to him like she usually did. He chuckled, stroking her messy curls back from her face.

'Did you sleep well?' he said.

'Hmm,' she hummed, closing her eyes.

He smiled. He was sure she was still half asleep whenever she snuck into his bed, but he didn't mind. It gave him time to think about how blessed he was to have a beautiful girl. A girl who still looked so much like her mother. But now, he could see the resemblance without feeling that ache in his chest he'd felt for so long. And he'd wager Brooke had something to do with that.

Sleep had been hard for him, now he knew what it was like to wake up with Brooke beside him. God, the two weeks it had been since that night had been torture for him. It was like having a taste of something incredibly addictive and not getting to enjoy it every chance he got. They'd talked about telling everyone—especially the kids, though, he half-suspected Gracie already knew—but decided on keeping it to themselves, for a little while, at least. To make sure, he supposed.

But he already was sure.

He wanted to shout it to the world, show everyone that Brooke was his, and he was hers. He wanted to hold her, kiss her, hold her gaze for that moment longer, regardless of who was around. But if she wasn't quite there, he'd give her time. She'd been burned before. It was only natural she might need more time than he did. Then again, he'd thought he'd never get to that point with anyone else. But the plain and simple truth was he was falling for Brooke, and he could no longer imagine a life without her. Without Maddie and Ollie.

His lease would be running out soon, and as far as he knew, so was hers. He was ready to dive in, head first. And if they were going to have any chance of seeing each other, spending as much time together as possible, they had to do something about it. They had to go all in.

Gracie's breathing evened out as she drifted back to sleep again, and he reached for his phone, opening up to their messages.

*Morning, beautiful.*

He waited a few minutes before he got her reply. A reply that was always the same when he sent his morning message, and it always brought a smile to his face.

*Morning, handsome.*

He tapped out another message. *Did you sleep well?*

A few more minutes passed and when he got one back, it was more incoherent than anything. He sighed, glancing over at Gracie, then slid out of the bed and headed towards the kitchen, dialling her number as he went.

'Hmm?' Brooke groaned.

He smiled. She must have still been half-asleep. His thoughts drifted back to waking up next to her, how he thought she was still one of the most beautiful things he'd ever seen, even as she slept. And her morning manner? Equally as cute. Even if she wasn't very talkative until she'd had coffee.

'Big night?' he teased, putting the kettle on.

'Mmm,' she hummed. 'Ollie forgot that sleep was a thing.'

Her words were drawn out, slow, and he pictured her laying in her bed with her eyes closed, her phone held to her ear. If he was there, he'd stroke her hair, holding her close until her eyes drifted open from the smell of coffee. She'd smile up at him the way she did the morning he woke up with her beside him. And the very thought he could have that every morning made his smile widen.

'Was he up all night?' he said. The housing situation could wait. Not only was it bad timing, since she'd had a bad night, but he wasn't going to suggest it over the phone. He wanted to see her face when he suggested it.

'Mhmm,' she hummed, clearly drifting in and out of sleep. 'All night,' she added slowly.

He bit the side of his cheek. Was today even the best day to mention it at all? He was sure it would be better timing once they were together. Once he had a chance to make her forget about her sleepless night, show her how easy it could be if they were together all the time.

He knew they hadn't known each other for very long, but why should it matter? He was a big believer in the whole you-just-know thing. He knew with Alice. And he knew with Brooke. He knew she was the one he wanted to wake up with every morning, that he didn't want to hide being with. He didn't want anyone else except for her. He just had to convince her of that.

'I'm sorry, love,' he said, serving up some coffee in his cup.

'It's not your fault,' she mumbled.

'Is he asleep now?'

'For now.'

He got the milk from the fridge. 'You should go back to sleep, then,' he said, decisively. He heard her hum again and knew she was already just about there. 'I'll come over in a bit and help out, okay?'

'Hmm.'

'Sweet dreams, Brooke.'

'Sweet dreams, Lewis,' she mumbled, drifting off again.

He smiled as he hung up the phone and thought about what he could bring over. Pancakes, perhaps. He might be able to get enough made before Gracie woke up again, or at least some. Then, he'd drop by the florist on his way over. If he was going to ask her today, he had to set the scene, after all. Besides, what harm could it do?

***

Lewis's words caught up to her in her delirious state. He's coming over? It was no surprise it made her smile, but why did she feel like he shouldn't? The smell of coffee wafted from the kitchen and it all came back to her. Lewis couldn't come over. Not now.

'N-no,' she mumbled into the phone. 'D-don't come over.' There was no response. *Damn it.* 'Lewis?'

She pulled the phone away from her ear to see the screen was black. God, he wasn't even still on the phone. She flicked to her previous calls list to see when he called. Half an hour ago. Half an hour had passed since he called. Damn it! Surely, she hadn't been *that* delirious, had she? Oh, what else did he say? She couldn't remember him saying a time he'd be coming over, but judging from when he came over last weekend, he wasn't far off. She flung herself off the bed and headed out of her room, ramming into Brett's chest when she turned into the hallway. She felt the wind knock out of her as though she'd walked into a brick wall. His chest was harder than she remembered. Then again, he had gotten a lot fitter since she last saw him.

He held onto her shoulders, keeping her upright. 'You okay, Brooke?'

She felt like her hallway was a lot smaller than it was. She felt flustered—and not in the same way she did when she was this close to Lewis. Her skin was prickling, and she struggled to steady her breaths.

'What are you doing here, Brett?' she blurted out.

He frowned. 'You wanted me to come over, remember?' he said. 'Ollie wasn't sleeping, and you wanted me to help. Ring any bells?'

She rubbed her forehead, feeling the blood rushing to her head from getting up so quickly. 'No, I mean *now*. Why are you *still* here?'

He shrugged. 'Figured I'd let you catch up on some sleep,' he said. 'Why? Is it a problem? Saturday's your day off, isn't it?'

She pushed past him, heading into the kitchen towards the smell of coffee. Hopefully, *that* would help her make better sense of things. 'I just … I have … plans,' she mumbled, beelining for the cup on the bench and taking a sip. She almost spat it back in the cup. 'What is *this*?'

'It's decaf,' he said. Her eyes widened. 'You drink too much coffee, Brooke. It's not good for you.'

'Like hell, it's not,' she said, her jaw feeling tense. 'Let me worry about what's good or bad for me.' She poured the fool's gold down the sink and rinsed her cup out, reaching for the jar of *real* coffee.

'You wanted my help, Brooke.'

'With the *kids*!' she said, spinning on her heel to face him. 'I needed help with the kids—*your* kids— because Ollie had me on the brink of insanity. Thank you for your help last night, but I'm fine now. And I certainly don't need you *helping* with anything else.' She waved the cup between them to make her point.

He stood up straighter, his jaw tensing. 'I thought ...' His words drifted off and he rubbed his eyes.

'Thought what, Brett? That you'd come back, and I'd forgive you and we'd go back to how we were?'

His stare was cold and distant. He looked over her, at a point somewhere above her head. She felt a weight in her chest and something stirred in her stomach—and not in a good way. She might have just been taking a stab in the dark when she said it, but it was *exactly* what he'd thought, wasn't it? She realised now she hadn't actually been expecting that. Hadn't she made her intentions clear when he came back?

'I—' she said, squeezing her eyes closed. 'I said it wasn't going to happen, Brett.'

'You've said that before,' he said, his voice sounding closer than it should be.

She opened her eyes slowly to find him standing only inches away. Too close for comfort. Her mind flicked back to the time he was referring to—before they first got together. Before kids. Before the heartache. He cupped her cheek and she felt the blood drain from her face. He wasn't going to kiss her, was he? He couldn't—surely, he wasn't *that* bad at reading her hints. Heck, they weren't even hints! She was straight out telling him it was not going to happen. But he was going to kiss her. She felt her heart racing and her breaths were choppy. He moved towards her and she couldn't help but think she just wanted to get out of there. And that Lewis would be there at any moment.

She turned her head and he stopped moving before his lips could touch her—clearly, he got *that* hint. 'You're right, Brett,' she whispered. 'I have said it before. And this time, I mean it.'

His hand dropped from her face and he took a step back. 'I guess I just thought ... since you asked for help ... you might change your mind.'

She shook her head, clutching the cup between her hands. 'I won't.'

'You can't be sure,' he said, stretching one hand towards her and running the other hand through his hair.

She opened her mouth to speak, but before anything came out, Maddie came into the kitchen and mumbled a greeting. 'Is Gracie coming over today?' she said.

'Mhmm,' Brooke hummed, hazarding a glance towards Brett. 'She is.'

'Who's Gracie?' Brett said, clearing his voice.

'Maddie's friend,' Brooke offered.

'And Lewis, too?' Maddie said, her eyes lighting up.

'Lewis?' Brett said, turning towards Brooke.

'Hmm? Probably,' she muttered, shrugging. She turned to make her coffee—and avoid eye contact with Brett.

'Oh, I hope he brings some food!' Maddie said, bouncing. 'What do you think he'll bring?'

'I … I don't know, honey,' she said, feeling the skin at the back of her neck prickle.

'Who's Lewis?' Brett repeated.

'Gracie's dad, duh,' Maddie said, rolling her eyes.

'Her dad, huh?' Brett said, his tone changing, reminding her of the days before he left. 'Does she have a mum?'

Brooke squeezed her eyes shut. 'Nope,' Maddie said. 'But she likes *my* mum and I think Lew—'

'*Maddie*,' Brooke said. 'Can you go get dressed? Gracie will be here soon.'

'Okay!' Maddie bounded off, and Brooke could feel Brett's eyes boring into her.

He barely waited until Maddie was out of the room before talking. 'So, Lewis?'

She sighed, continuing making her coffee. Why should it be an issue? She had already told Brett it wasn't going to happen between them. He had no right to be jealous. At all. Ever. 'Yes, Lewis,' she muttered.

'You and L—' he started.

'Me and Lewis,' she finished.

'How … how long?'

'It's new,' she said. 'A couple weeks before you came back.'

'Is it serious?' Why did he sound almost ... hurt?

'I think so,' she said, sighing. She took a sip of her coffee that was *finally* made. 'You should ... umm ... you should leave.'

He nodded slowly. 'I agree,' he muttered, gathering his things off the table.

'This doesn't change anything, Brett,' she said. He responded simply by looking at her—past her— again. 'With the kids. I'd still like you to be more involved with them if that's what you want.'

He nodded slowly, straightening himself. 'Goodbye, Brooke.'

'Bye, Brett.'

***

Lewis grabbed the insulated bag and bunch of flowers from the car and followed Gracie towards the house, his heart pounding as it always did when he thought of Brooke. Except this time was a little different. This time, he was going to suggest they move in together—something that was a huge decision for any couple, let alone one that involved kids. Would she agree? Would she see it as the next logical step like he did?

He thought she would. At least, he hoped she would. Surely, she felt the same as he did, didn't she? Gracie had just bounced up the steps—he wasn't far behind—when the front door swung open and he realised Brooke wasn't alone. He halted, but Gracie didn't seem to notice. She raced past the man to start bouncing and telling Maddie something about pancakes, bacon, and ice cream. Well, there goes his surprise. He considered the man, his jaw clenched. He was the same man he'd seen leaving the house a few weeks ago—Brett. He knew Brooke was letting him see the kids. And though he wasn't exactly pleased she'd be spending time with her ex, he knew it was her choice. One he'd have to get used to.

But this time seemed different. This time, there was something about Brett's manner that seemed off. He seemed disappointed, jealous, even. Or maybe he was imagining it. His clothes were worn as if he hadn't just thrown them on in the last few hours. Lewis shifted his gaze to Brooke who gave him a weak smile. She was in her pyjamas still, looking sexy as hell, her arms folded defensively across her chest. Brett cleared his throat, touching Brooke's arm in a way that Lewis wanted to be the only man to touch her like, and headed down the steps, pausing only a brief moment next to him.

'Lewis,' he said gruffly.

'Brett,' Lewis responded.

Brett's eyes narrowed, and he glanced back at Brooke, who was now leaning against the door frame, her body tense, and nodded. He glanced at Lewis once more and continued walking to his car— the car that Lewis didn't recognise, which only served to annoy him more. How had he not realised

Brett's car was parked there? After all, Lewis had parked right behind it! He really needed to pay more attention to cars he encountered.

He glanced back towards Brooke, still finding it difficult to move his feet. She smiled weakly again, walking slowly towards him and planting her lips on his in a quick kiss. A kiss he felt like there was more to, unless he was just being sceptical, paranoid.

'Everything okay?' she said, hesitantly, her brow furrowed.

It wasn't until then he realised he hadn't kissed her back. 'You tell me.' Though, he wasn't sure he wanted to know.

'What's that supposed to mean?' she said quietly, dropping her gaze, her shoulders lifting.

He felt his jaw tense. Was that how it was always going to be with matters concerning Brett? Heck, the guy shows up out of nowhere after spending so long without contact and sends *his* girlfriend into being defensive and secretive? How else could he react?

'He looked tired,' he pointed out. 'Was Ollie the only one keeping you up last night?'

He saw her body tense, and she glanced back at the house, but not at him. 'Can we talk about this later?' she said, her voice still quiet.

His hands felt heavy—heck, all of him felt heavy—and his throat burned. 'No, I don't think we can.'

'Lewis,' she said, finally looking at him. Her eyes were saddened and glistened with unshed tears.

'Why was he here, Brooke?'

She opened her mouth to say something, then snapped it closed, biting into her lip. What was she going to say that she decided not to? What changed without him realising?

'He, umm,' she muttered, dropping her gaze. 'He stayed the night.'

A straight-up punch would have been better. His chest tightened, and he felt like the wind got knocked out of him. He *stayed* the night? Seems he'd been reading too far into it all along, which only justified him avoiding relationships for the last five years. Brooke wasn't the woman he thought. He'd thought, since she'd been cheated on, that it wasn't something she would do to him. Seems he was wrong about that, too. His whole body felt tense, and like it was going to fall apart at the same time. He had to leave. He couldn't deal with losing someone he cared about again. Not like this. But he had. She was always going to be Brett's. He was just a stand-in while he was gone.

'Gracie!' he yelled towards the house.

Brooke clasped a hand over her mouth, her other hand clutching to his arm. 'Lewis, *please*,' she said, shaking her head slowly. 'It's not what you think.'

'What the hell is *that* supposed to mean?' he said, turning back to her.

'Nothing happened!' she shrieked. 'God, I shouldn't have to defend myself every time the *father of my children* shows up.'

'Then, don't,' he said flatly. '*Gracie!*'

'I called him, okay?' she said, a tear rolling down

her cheek. Another followed suit on her other side. 'Ollie wouldn't sleep. I was desperate. I called him.'

'In the middle of the night?'

'He wanted to be more involved with them, so I'm letting him be more involved with them.'

'By being your lifeline?'

'You would do the same thing!'

He shook his head, feeling another stab in his chest. 'No, I wouldn't,' he growled. 'Because *my* wife is *dead*. Or have you forgotten that little fun fact?' He knew his voice was dripping with sarcasm, but he didn't care. '*Gracie!*'

'Right,' she said, her voice shaky. 'You wouldn't have taken a second glance at me if she was still here.'

He shook his head slowly. 'That was a low blow, Brooke.'

She swallowed, more tears rolling down her cheeks as she stared at the ground. Her body was shaking, and he didn't know what to think anymore. 'But it's true,' she whispered.

He swallowed the lump in his own throat. 'You know, I had this picture in my head,' he said flatly, his eyes burning as much as his throat. 'That we'd move in together, be a family. You'd be Gracie's mother, and I'd be Maddie and Ollie's father. It didn't matter that it's not biological. It would be the five of us, and we'd rely only on each other.' She lifted her gaze to meet his, her lips parted. Her heart breaking. Like his. '*I* wanted to be the person you called for help, Brooke, not the other guy.' Her lips quivered, and he wished it didn't have to be this way. But she'd made her choice when she called Brett instead of him.

'*What*, Dad?' Gracie said, oblivious to the whole exchange going on between him and Brooke.

'Get in the car, Gracie,' he said. 'We're going.'

'But—'

'Lewis,' Brooke whispered, swiping at her eyes.

'*Get in the car,*' he repeated. Gracie sighed, said her goodbyes and dragged herself slowly towards the car. He shoved the flowers and bag in Brooke's arms. 'These were for you, so you may as well keep them.'

'Lewis,' she said again.

'Goodbye, Brooke.'

# Chapter 16

Brooke stared at the flowers on her table, swiping another tear from her eyes. How had things gone so wrong? All because of one delirious, *stupid* decision! It made sense to her to call Brett last night. Lewis couldn't have come over as easily as Brett could—he had Gracie. He had a kid of his own. She wouldn't have subjected him to a sleepless night, knowing he had to deal with his own kid the next day. Brett had no one else to worry about. He could go home and sleep all day if he wanted to.

He was their father.

Her thoughts drifted back to what Lewis said, about the picture he had of them. Of being a family. She'd wanted it, too. Heck, she'd thought she was thinking of it too soon, but clearly, he had been, too.

If she could have picked who could be the real father of her children, she would have chosen Lewis all along. But the choice was never really hers. And it never would be.

Brett was their father. He always would be, and she couldn't change that. Then again, even if she'd wanted to, she wouldn't have Maddie and Ollie if it wasn't for Brett. She wouldn't have met Lewis if things had worked out with Brett. And if she hadn't met Lewis, she wouldn't be hurting right now. Life would just go on as usual, with the exception that Brett would be back. But she wouldn't have fallen for an incredible guy so quickly, then had her heart broken. She blamed Brett for that, too.

Ollie shrieked, bringing her back to the present, and flipped his plate on the floor, spreading bits of pancake everywhere. The pancakes Lewis made. She couldn't bring herself to eat anything—she was sure it would just come back up again. But the kids, at least, were enjoying the pancakes. She had to talk to him. She couldn't wait and let the burn simmer longer. She knew, without a doubt, her life wouldn't be the same without him. They might have said things to each other that hurt, but she was sure it wasn't something they couldn't work through. They just had to work through it together. Maybe the hour or so it had been since he left was enough for him to cool off a little. At least she hoped it would be.

She heard the lock of her front door click and knew that was her cue. Suddenly, she wasn't as sure as she was before. She heard Georgie's shoes tapping down the hallway towards the kitchen, and Maddie's eyes lit up.

'Aunty Georgie!' she shrieked, sliding off her chair and launching herself into Georgie's arms.

'Hey, sweetpea!' she said, giving her a hug and planting a kiss on Ollie's head. 'What are we having?'

'Pancakes! Lewis brought them over,' Maddie said, settling herself back in her seat. 'But then he had to go.'

Georgie lifted her eyebrow at Brooke. 'Ah, I see,' she mumbled. 'You look like he—'

'Thanks for coming over, Georgie,' Brooke interrupted, making a mental note she had to remind her what words were not to be used around the kids.

'Of course,' Georgie said. 'Go fix everything up. We'll be fine.'

Brooke did as she was told, jumping in the car and driving towards Lewis's house. He wasn't expecting her. Nor would he likely want to see her. But she had to see him. She couldn't just let things end this way without him knowing. And she couldn't let it end on such a bad note. She pulled up at his place but stayed in the car. His car wasn't there. He wasn't home. She squeezed her eyes shut. What was she supposed to do now? Wait until he came home? What if he was hours away? She thought if he was going to be anywhere, he would have been home.

She swiped at another stupid tear and sighed, heading back home. Or, at least, down a road she thought would lead her home, but only made her realise she wasn't as familiar with this side of town as she thought. So, why did it look familiar? After a few minutes of driving, she took another turn and realised why it looked familiar—this was the street his mother lived on. It was worth a shot, right? But what if he wasn't there, either? Then again, what if he was? What would she do then?

She pulled over in front of Gladys's house, behind a white ute—his car—and felt her heart skip a beat. He was here. Now, what? She forced herself to climb out of her car and walk slowly up to the door. What was she supposed to say? Chances are, Gladys would answer the door since it was her house. She lifted her hand and dropped it back to her side before knocking.

Gladys didn't know she and Lewis had been ... involved. How was she supposed to explain why she was there? She could ask if she left something after the party, she supposed. Though, it had been well over a month since then. Even if she *had* left something, chances are Gladys wouldn't still have it. She took a step backwards and halted. She couldn't leave. Not now. What were the odds of accidentally showing up at the place where Lewis happened to be when she was supposed to be on her way back home? She was never really one to believe in signs, but if she was, she'd take that as a sign.

She would just have to be brave. If Gladys answered, she would simply ask if Lewis was there. Perhaps, even, Lewis might realise it was her at the door and save her from having to explain anything at all. Maybe. She took a deep breath to try to work up the courage to knock, but quickly felt that courage dwindling. This was ridiculous. *She* was ridiculous. If she believed in signs, wouldn't Brett's timing of showing up at her house as she was leaving to see Lewis have been one, too? Things weren't going to happen with Brett, of course. But wouldn't it be like keeping her away from Lewis? Maybe things were never supposed to happen with him. Maybe it was simply to get her back out in the dating world—to give her courage to love again.

She startled as the door swung open and she came face-to-face with those blue-green eyes and thick eyelashes she'd found it easy to fall for, the square jaw accentuated with the perfectly trimmed three-day growth, the lips that still lingered everywhere they touched. Who was she kidding? She didn't believe in signs. The truth was, she could no longer imagine living without this guy. In the short time since he left her house and seeing him now, she'd gone through emotional hell. And the only way to fix that was by being in his arms again. Even if she had to beg.

The warmth in his eyes disappeared in the split second it took for him to realise she was there, his lips pressing into a thin line. He had his keys and a piece of paper in his hands, a list, by the looks of it.

'Lewis,' she whispered, shakily, twisting her hands together.

He glanced back into the house and stepped outside, closing the door behind him. 'What are you doing here, Brooke?'

There was no warmth in his voice, and it sent a chill down her spine. She felt a whole lot smaller than she knew she was, but she wasn't going to leave until she said what she had to say.

'Looking for you,' she said. 'I think we should talk.'

He scoffed. 'Haven't we talked enough?'

'Please?'

He studied her for a moment, then ran a hand through his hair, closing his eyes. 'Fine,' he said finally, opening his eyes. 'Go ahead.'

She took a shaky breath, half surprised he was even giving her a chance to talk, and also, suddenly at a loss for words. 'I'm sorry,' she said slowly. 'I really am. For saying … about Alice … and not calling. I guess I … I don't know. I was … selfish, I suppose. And tired. And I wanted to see if Brett was really going to be true to his word.'

His eyebrow lifted, and she realised she was blurting out things she hadn't even realised were true. But it all made sense. In a way, she was testing Brett without realising it. Part of her wanted him to fail that test—the part that wanted to know she was right, that he couldn't handle the kids by himself. The other part of her wanted him to do as well as he did, for her kids.

'I didn't … realise … that's what I was doing. I think part of me wanted to … to get back at Brett for not making an effort sooner,' she said, dropping her gaze to the ground between them. Her eyes were burning, and her heart felt like it was being torn out of her chest. 'And I guess I thought, because you have Gracie, you couldn't have easily come over to help me.'

'I would have been over in a heartbeat,' he said softly. The coldness wasn't as obvious, but he was still holding back.

'I know, now,' she continued, risking a glance up at him. He was focussed on her, and she couldn't read his expression. She sighed, wondering if she'd ever learn to read his expressions. If he'd ever give her the chance to. 'I was exhausted, Lewis, and stressed, and I wasn't coping. And I—I didn't want you to ... to see that p—part of me, in case you ... you—' she broke off, swiping at her wet cheeks. It was getting harder and harder to talk and she felt like she was digging herself deeper into a hole.

'In case I changed my mind,' he said, almost so quietly she almost didn't hear it.

She squeezed her eyes shut, feeling the fat tears roll down her cheeks, and nodded. It seemed sillier now it had been spoken aloud. Why would she think he'd change his mind when he saw her at her worst? Heck, her worst occurred in the middle of the night and it was directly related with her kids. Sure, someone who didn't have a kid might not understand, but surely, he'd had his days with Gracie. Maybe he couldn't relate to the intensity having two kids provides, but he had to handle Gracie on his own, from the start. She at least had Brett—and the little help he'd been—when she had Maddie.

'Brooke.'

He said it softly, and there was no hint of the coldness anymore. In fact, it was somewhat saddened, yet comforting at the same time. She looked up at him again, her heart skipping a beat at the battle he seemed to be having with himself. Was he going to give her another chance? But surely, she had to explain herself more! God, if she was in his shoes, she'd probably need a whole lot more convincing than what she just gave him. Then again, maybe that's one of the things she loved about him.

***

He didn't need much convincing. Not when it was Brooke. Sure, he'd been surprised to see her there—at his mother's place—waiting to talk to him. But he hadn't heard a knock, and going from the surprised look on her face, she hadn't expected him to open the door when he did. Then again, he completely understood why she might have hesitated in knocking. What if his mother answered?

Heck, he was even worried about his mother simply seeing who was at the door before he had a chance to close it. It was only a coincidence he was ducking out of the house to pick up some groceries for his mother and she happened to be there. Truth is, the short time it had been since he saw her that morning had seemed to stretch on for days. His heart had been aching, and he couldn't help but think he'd overreacted. Had he?

She'd called her ex up to help her in her time of need instead of him. Then again, he could see why she thought Brett was more available to help than he was. Brett had already seen her worst. He'd lived with her for years, had kids with her. And then he left. He had to remember that. Brett might have come over to help her last night, but he *left* when Brooke would have needed him most. And, according to Brooke, he'd had a lot of years of not being much help. Lewis would be different—he *was* different. He'd never been the kind of guy to run away. And he wasn't going to start now.

He pulled her into his arms and held her close. He could feel her sobbing against his chest, her body shaking. He cupped the back of her head with his hand, stroking her hair.

'It was s—stupid,' she sobbed, shaking her head. 'I was stupid. I wasn't th—thinking. I'm s—sorry.'

He shushed her, pressing a kiss to the top of her head. How could he not forgive her? He'd never felt that anything was more right than having Brooke in his arms. Heck, he wasn't even sure it had felt so right with Alice, though it had been so long since he'd held her. Alice might have been his past, but he knew Brooke was his future. And he was going to do everything he could to make sure it stayed that way.

'I need you, Lewis,' she whispered, pressing her face harder against his chest. He felt his heart skip a beat. 'And I—I want to be a ... family ... with you.' She lifted her face towards his, her eyes puffy and glistening, her cheeks wet. But she was beautiful. 'If you'll give me another chance.'

He closed the gap between them, pressing his lips to hers in a combination of love, forgiveness, and pure need. It was wet, it was sappy, but he didn't care. Because feeling her lips on his and knowing they had another chance at happiness made it the most beautiful kiss he'd ever had. She broke the kiss, looking up at him, her lips curved up in a smile, her brow creased.

'Is that a yes?' she said.

His lips curved up to mirror hers. 'Damn right it is,' he said, pressing his lips against hers again. Her lips parted to let him in and he kissed her deeply, thoroughly, taking as much as he could that was socially acceptable in public. Though, he wished he could have more.

The front door swung open and they jumped apart, but he knew his mother saw all she needed to see. Brooke dropped her gaze, her cheeks flushing, and he tried to hide the smile creeping onto his face. Why did he feel like a teenage boy that just got busted making out with his girlfriend?

Gladys squinted, shifting her gaze between the two of them, then sighed. 'Well, it's about bloody time,' she said, folding her arms across her chest, smiling.

'*Mother*!' he said, feigning shock.

Gladys raised her eyebrows. 'What? I'm not the only *meddling mother*, you know,' she said, nodding towards Brooke. 'Lily is just as much to blame as I am.'

'So, you and my mother worked *together* to set us up?' Brooke said, her brow creasing again.

'That's right,' Gladys said, a proud look on her face.

'You threw a *party*!' Lewis pointed out.

Gladys nodded. 'Well, I wasn't going to let you get with any of those hussies, was I? We just figured we had to put you both in a place where you can meet and see if it happened naturally.'

He squinted, and he saw Brooke's mouth drop open. So, they were set up. Who cares? They could feign being mad at their parents, but the truth was, they wouldn't have met otherwise. And he couldn't imagine *not* having Brooke in his life anymore. Gladys flashed a triumphant smile and went back inside. He focussed back on Brooke. She squinted from the brightness of the sun, her lips pressed together in a smile as she looked up at him.

'Well,' he said, clearing his throat. 'That takes care of telling our parents.' He took hold of her hands and pulled her closer.

'You do realise we were set up, right?' she teased. 'By our *mothers*?'

'Mhmm,' he hummed, pressing a kiss to her right cheek, her forehead, her left cheek. 'But only the first meeting,' he added. 'Definitely not the second, or third.' He kissed her nose and rested his forehead against hers.

'Mmm, but the kids had a big part in the playdates,' she said, rubbing her nose against his.

'And our date?' he added. 'And *after* our date?

That was on us.' He kissed her again.

'Mmm,' she hummed against his lips. 'That *was* on us, wasn't it?'

He nodded and kissed her again, not holding anything back, because he knew, set up or not, he would spend forever with her in his arms. And it was the happiest he'd been in a long time—ever, perhaps.

'I love you, Brooke Cottle,' he said, holding her tightly.

'I love you, Lewis Rieder,' she said, flicking her eyes up at him, peeking through her long lashes. Something mischievous flashed through her eyes and her lips quirked up to one side. He felt her body press against his, making his senses come alive. 'Hmm … Rieder,' she said seductively. 'Ride … me?'

His eyebrows flicked up and he felt his body tense. 'Oh, I will,' he said, drawing out the syllables.

He swept her up into his arms and carried her to his car, plopping her giggling body in the passenger seat, and raced around to the driver side, jumping in and firing up the ignition. The groceries would have to wait.

There was something he had to take care of first.